≈ ≈
SAINT

Also by Christine Bell

The Perez Family

SAINT

Christine Bell

W. W. Norton & Company
New York • London

The author gratefully acknowledges permission to quote from
"DUENO DE NADA" by Manual Alejandro and Ana Magdalena
Copyright © Ediciones Musicales RCA Espanola, S.A., Madrid

Manufacturing by the Haddon Craftsmen, Inc.

Library of Congress Cataloging-in-Publication Data
Bell, Christine.
Saint.
I. Title.
PS3552.E489S26   1985   813´.54 85-12256

ISBN 0-393-31350-6

W. W. Norton & Company, Inc.
500 Fifth Avenue, New York, N.Y. 10110
W. W. Norton & Company Ltd.
10 Coptic Street, London WC1A 1PU

Printed in the United States of America

1 2 3 4 5 6 7 8 9 0

With special thanks to The Family,
the DePietros, N. Devany, I. Fiallos Finstad, M. Newman,
S. Naranjo Webber and the continued inspiration of
the Madame, Ouida Louise Duganne.

Dueño de ti,
dueño de qué;
dueño de nada.
...Dueño del aire
y del reflejo
da la luna sobre el agua;
dueño de nada.

≈ ≈
SAINT

PART I
Santa del Rio,
South America

If heat had a smell, it would smell like this: layers upon layers of rotting vegetation steaming on the jungle floor. It is not an unpleasant odor by itself. It rises bestial and musklike. But in the hot moist air before the rains come, the jungle tries to cover it like a whore with sickening sweet wafts of frangipani and Spanish jasmine.

If heat had a sound, it would be this manic staccato of unseen birds and the on-again, off-again static of insects.

If heat had a vision, it is here now. The old yellow dog lies at my feet, his body vibrating with quick pants. His tongue out. His eyes suppliant. His mistress is dying. He is not allowed in the sick room, so he has taken to my heels. There is no comfort for him. No one can save the Señora and nothing but rain will save us from the heat. My pats only serve to make the old dog hotter and he turns from them. I talk to him constantly. Perhaps that is why he moves when I move. He lies at my feet when I sit. I fill his water bowl and sit with him when he drinks. If I fill it and move away, he follows me without touching it.

The air is heavy enough to hold in your hand. It should be cooler inside. The paths from the main gate leading to the stables and the main house are clean and neat. The low kept ground cover appears cool and green. The iced chandeliers inside, the open windows and polished wooden floors, the crystal vases and silver tea sets appropriately spaced in the large rooms, the fans droning discreetly in every room, in every corridor—yes, it should be cooler inside. But this is the kind of heat that has substance, that clings and speaks. This is the kind of heat that knows the convoluted corridors of the house as well as it knows the jungle outside.

We live in Santa del Rio, not in the city proper where I have my business, but on one of the largest haciendas in the district—a district which is jungle, barely inhabitable, surrounded by jungle, which is uninhabitable. I do not know how large the hacienda is or where its boundaries lie. Except that it seems very small now that the Señora has come home to die and we do not go any farther from the main house than to the stables or the garden pathways. I have been here for fifteen years, not always in this same spot, imprisoned by the house and the heat. It is too hot to sit in one place for any length of time. It is too hot not to sit for any length of time.

I sat at the kitchen table turning the pages of an outdated fashion magazine, the old dog at my feet. My sister-in-law Rosa was sitting at the other end of the table sweating. It made me hotter just to look at her. I wished she would do something aside from just sitting there sweating and was about to tell her so when a man appeared in the doorway like a vapor. He had coarse stringy hair, the color of fire, streaming to his waist where it met more orange string covering his body to his knees. His legs and chest were bare. It wasn't strings of fiery hair at all but some sort of dyed palm grass decorating his body. He was old and strong. He was definitely not one of the locals, but he stood fixed in the doorway as if he had always been there.

"Dear God," Rosa said, "the jungle has grown into the house!"

The man did not seem to understand. The little housemaid came out from behind the man.

"I will get Ada," she said. "I do not understand his dialect."

"Sit down, sir," I said, gesturing to the chair, as Rosa seemed incapable of any more speech. He did not sit down. He did not move.

Our housekeeper came a minute later. Ada is Indian, but not Indian like that man was Indian. She didn't appear to know the man. They spoke in a dialect I had never heard before.

"What does he want, Ada?" I finally interrupted.

"Wait, Rubia, I am getting the story now."

She began a moment later: "His name is Yaguato. He says that he is the leader of one of the tribes far away. He says that he comes personally because when he was a young man, he met the Señora when she was inspecting her land and she was very kind to his people."

"He lives here on the hacienda?" I said.

"No," Ada said. "He lives in the jungle on land belonging to you or rather to the hacienda. He says that he has traveled for twelve days. First his people came with him by foot and canoe through the jungle to a village where he traded mats to a man on one of the cargo ships for passage down river to Santa del Rio. The river was very swift, he says, but his feet are old and very slow coming here and he hopes that the Señora is still alive because he has brought medicine for her."

"He walked from town?" I said. "That's forty minutes by jeep."

"I'm sure he knows how far away it is," Ada said.

"I did not mean it to be disrespectful," I said. "Only that I am amazed."

"Should I tell him that?"

"Not in those words, please. Tell him that the Señora is still alive and that we are most appreciative and honored by his long journey."

Ada spoke to him and he replied while untying a little leather pouch which had been hidden in the strings of his grass skirt. Ada turned to Rosa who was still in a catatonic sweat and said, "He wants to know which one of you he should give the medicine to. I told him that you are the daughter of the Señora, but that Rubia is the daughter-in-law and is in charge of the medicine."

"Tell him to keep his medicine," Rosa said. "Tell him that only *our* God can save my mother now."

"Please, Ada, don't translate that! Tell him that I will be honored to take the medicine," I said.

Ada spoke to the man. He moved for the first time from his spot in the doorway and handed me the leather pouch.

"Please thank him for me and please ask what are the instructions."

"Aren't you carrying it a little too far, Rubia?" Rosa said.

I was not asking instructions to be polite. I didn't know if Rosa was aware that I often mixed a pinch or two of the local cures in with the medicine from the doctor for the Señora. Doctor Garcia said that nothing could hurt the Señora now and who knows what might help.

Ada told me that the man said I should mix this much (she held her thumb and forefinger a half-inch apart) in water and give it to the Señora whenever she could swallow.

"Ask him how he knew the Señora was sick. Ask him if they have cancer in his tribe, Ada. Ask if he wants food or wants to rest. Tell him that we can drive him back to town tomorrow or when he likes, to catch his boat."

They spoke.

"He says that he will return the same way he came."

And the man turned and left.

"Ada," I said, "how did you know his language? Is that where you come from? What else did he say? Who was he?"

"He didn't say anything else. He is a very great man if he is who I think he is. I didn't come from where he comes from. He is from very deep in the jungle, but the dialect he speaks is very similar to the language my grandparents spoke. A very great man...but of course Rosa is right—I'm sure he's not baptized."

"Who cares," I said.

Ada crossed herself reverently at my blasphemy and sighed, "*Dios mio.*"

"Wait," I said, as she turned to leave. "Does he have cancer where he comes from?"

"Well, it is hard to translate the name he calls it. Literally, it means 'the curse of the wood which rots from the inside.' "

At that, Rosa took the little leather pouch sitting on the table in front of me and poured it down the sink running the water over it.

"My mother is not wood that rots from the inside," she said.

I looked into the sink. There was not a trace left. I could have killed her then. I could have moved through the heat and strangled her.

"Twelve fucking days," I screamed in English, pounding the table. "Twelve fucking days that man travels and you pour the fucking holy medicine down the sink 'cause he's not Catholic and you don't like his fucking medical terminology."

Rosa speaks little English, but she must have understood the "fucking."

"Stop cursing," she yelled back in Spanish. (Ada crossed herself.) "How dare you curse when my mother is dying! You are always cursing!"

It wasn't funny I know, but I started laughing. I started laughing uncontrollably. I started laughing like the horrible screeching of the unseen birds in the jungle. If heat could speak it would sound like I did laughing.

2

≈ ≈ ≈ ≈ ≈ ≈ ≈ ≈ ≈ ≈ ≈

W e have suspended time to prevent the Señora from dying. Each day is an eternity. Each second of that eternity is as dense as the heat.
I married into this family fifteen years ago, when my husband was a foreign exchange student in New York. I have been here ever since. I can't remember any of the years being so hot, but it must be like this every year before the rains come. I barely had enough Spanish the first year I was here to ask the Señora if we could afford air-conditioning. I was being sarcastic—the grillwork on the front door probably cost enough to air-condition all of Santa del Rio—but I was already using "we" when it came to terms of finance.

"That is not the point, Rubia," she said. "You must become acclimated. We are as much a part of the jungle as we are of this house. That is not what needs to be changed to become modern."

Perhaps I did become acclimated for I remember it being cool last year. I remember being a part of the small dark circle which marks us on the map. But everything is disturbed in this heat, like vapor rising from the ground to distort the landscape.

I have been thinking lately. By thinking, I mean that I translate each part of our existence from Spanish into English in order to clarify, to understand, to regain some aborted identity. The smallest things take on huge amounts of thought. I

8

am beginning to wish for Anglo food and can no longer understand why everything is so mixed up down here, the peas and rice and meat all thrown together in one big heap on the plate. The water goes down the sink backwards. There are upside-down question marks at the beginning of sentences even when they are spoken.

I could just as well think in Spanish—I have for many years—but the Spanish words taste foreign in my mouth now. I wander about thinking aloud to myself in English when it gets too hot to sit still. ("Who are you talking to, Mama?" my younger daughter asked. "To Pepe," I told her. "But he's only a dog and doesn't understand English," she said.)

I feel stranger and more Anglo everyday. My hair seems blonder. My eyes, bluer. My body, longer and thinner.

When I grow tired of thinking, sometimes I pray to Santa del Rio, the patron saint of this city, the name of the city. Not out loud, not even in front of Pepe out loud. If anyone heard me praying out loud here, they would think I was taking God's name in vain. I was brought up Catholic also, but not Catholic the way they are Catholic.

Dear Santa del Rio, I pray in Spanish, but that sounds like I am praying to the whole district of city and jungle, of land and river.

Dear Saint of the River, I pray in English. But it is too precise in English and no one really knows who the saint of the river is. It is generally thought to be the Blessed Virgin. So I try Hail Marys to the Blessed Virgin in Spanish and in English, but that Mary doesn't sound as all-encompassing as the Santa del Rio.

Anyway, I pray to the Santa del Rio because I love the Señora and she is dying. All communication is valid.

3

There is much tension in this house. The usual peace, or rather the truce which had evolved over many years, has been broken.

The usual chores necessary to run the hacienda have been suspended or reassigned to the Indian "farmhands." This was fine three months before when the Señora entered the hospital again and life centered around the hospital. But since the Señora decided to spend her last days at home, it has left both my husband and his father idle and underfoot in the main house.

I am also idle and underfoot since it would be unthinkable that I attend to my usual business. I own and manage a lingerie store in the old part of the city. All the more unthinkable since everyone in this house considers my store an eccentric and embarrassing hobby, although for many years it has been my way of keeping sane.

My three nieces and two daughters are also idle and underfoot. I thought that they were on some kind of usual midterm break (I have always had a little trouble comprehending their grade and vacation system here), but when I questioned them, Rosa's three girls looked horrified, Patricia giggled, and Margherita rolled her eyes and said, "Mama, it is not possible that you call this a vacation when our grandmother is dying." The girls need to be quieted often since their reaction to such an adult situation as their grandmother's dying is to giggle uncontrollably at the slightest provocation.

Juan Ortega, Rosa's husband, is, on the other hand, busy sulking because he had to cancel three dancing engagements. He is a professional flamenco dancer trained in Spain and usually spends about six months out of the year away on dancing engagements—parades, festivals and nightclubs. Sometimes Rosa and their children accompany him on shorter trips, but more often they stay here. He is also busy sulking because even he would not dare engage in his usual activity when he is not dancing, which is the only activity he pursues while he is home, which is whoring.

Aside from going to church, Rosa's normal activity when she is not away with her husband is trying to persuade her husband that she should be away with him and trying to persuade him that they should all live far away from here permanently where the weather would be better and where he could get a regular job.

"If we lived where it was not always so hot, if my husband had his own house, if he were a salesman in a store," Rosa says, "these things would not happen."

By "these things," I take it she means stray young females showing up at the door pregnant, pretty second cousins blushing under his touch when he condescends to dance with them at local fiestas, and strange women in too-tight dresses approaching him on the street with "*Oye Chico!* Remember me?"

And Rosa, ah dear Rosa—she is far from idle and far from sulking. She is sweating with responsibility. She is everywhere at once and nowhere at all. She supervises, directs, organizes, aids, like a saint in religious heat. Even when she just sits and sweats, the wheels of responsibility are turning in her head. Sometimes I hear a cluck of her tongue when the wheel hits a rut. If sweat had a sound, it would be Rosa's tongue clucking.

For a person who has spent her life trying to get away or praying to get away or persuading others to take her away, she has done quite a turnaround. She is never far from hand. First, she takes away our usual duties in order to "organize" them. Then she assigns them back to us. Then she takes them away again because she says that we are not doing them correctly and then she complains that no one helps her. This pattern not only extends to the immediate family and household but also to visiting doctors, visiting nurses from the visiting nurse service, visiting priests, visiting workers from the hacienda, visiting neighbors, and plain visitors. They bring fruit and prayers, cures and flowers.

"If you please, mix the medicine now," Rosa told me after dinner, the day she threw out the cure from the old Indian.

"That is what I am doing now," I said. It was obvious enough, for I was sitting at the kitchen table with all the medicinal ingredients and jars, measuring cups, directions, droppers and vials. I continued mixing where I had left off.

"What are you doing!" Rosa screamed as she watched. "Trying to poison my mother?"

"You dumped the poison down the sink, remember?"

"But that is not the same thing I think you usually put in now. That is not even from one of the jars the doctor gave you."

"No, this is a teaspoonful of the cure sent by Ada's second cousin who is not only baptized, but is a godchild of the Señora's."

"And who gave you permission to include this teaspoonful from this cure?"

"The doctor."

"Which doctor?"

"Doctor Garcia—the Señora's doctor, our family's doctor." The same doctor who said three months ago that the Señora would not live more than one month. But I did not mention this to Rosa.

"If you please, I cannot believe this."

"Then you must believe that I am lying and that I am trying to poison your mother."

"That is not what I said."

"Then what are you saying?"

Her tongue clucked.

"Look Rosa, if you prefer to mix the medicine yourself, then please come right ahead."

"You know I do not have a mind for chemistry and that my English is not good enough to follow the directions."

"Well?" I said.

"I asked you to do it. I cannot do everything around here by myself."

It was by default that I was chosen to mix the medicine in the first place. There were strenuous objections mostly by Rosa, and I had to agree with her that the constant stream of doctors and nurses here would be far more capable of performing such an important task. But the directions for the medicine, which came from the cancer specialist in Lima who had done research in England, came to our family doctor here in Saint in English and that is my native tongue, so we had "no choice" as Rosa said.

I did take a required science course in college and there are only four ingredients to mix, two of which are drinking alcohol and corn syrup, so it is not a difficult task.

I have come to enjoy mixing the medicine, so I have not told Rosa that, in the half page of Latin medical hieroglyphics, these "English" directions contain only four words that are in English: "mix," "in," "the," and "patient." Doctor Garcia helped me to get over my initial paranoia at the task by explaining the ingredients to me. He said that a drop or two more or less of the medicinal components, morphine and cocaine, would not help or hurt the Señora. He also assured me that a drop or two of the local cures—Ada had been hysterical that her second cousin's brew was not the drug of choice—also would not hurt to mix in.

"The Señora is only still alive by her will, and the will of God, of course," Doctor Garcia said looking a little put off by the fact that the Señora had seemingly disregarded his own prediction that she would not last another day some two months ago. "This new medicine is only revolutionary in the idea of patient comfort, not of cure, Rubia. It will not cure her. It doesn't matter how much corn syrup you put in. The alcohol does not matter too much either. Also, if the Señora seems too lethargic, it would be fine if you put an extra drop of cocaine in, and if the Señora seems too anxious or is thrashing about, you leave out a drop of the cocaine and add a drop of morphine. And a drop or so of the local medicine could also do nothing to harm her..."

"But if I translated the English part of the directions into Spanish, why couldn't one of the nurses mix it?"

"They could, of course. But technically, the nurses only administer the medicine and the doctor or pharmacist prepares it, but I cannot be here all the time and you know what it's like waiting for medicine at the pharmacy in town. This way you can regulate her daily dose and it is a good idea to have one of the family actively participate in the care of the patient. You are quite capable. But if you would *prefer* not to..."

"No, I want to. I'm just afraid of getting it wrong and hurting her."

"This medicine cannot hurt her or cure her, Rubia. It is only to help her get a good night's sleep without drugging her into a coma."

And so I have become the high priestess of the medicine, much to Rosa's dismay. It is the only thing I do by myself with love for the Señora without outside interference. I understand that it is not a cure, but the word "revolutionary" used by

Doctor Garcia has transformed me into an avid chemist.

The half page of directions for the medicine is labeled "Brinkston's Cocktail." I serve it in a fine stemmed crystal glass on a lace doily on a silver tray, like a cool drink to refresh the Señora.

4

≈ ≈ ≈ ≈ ≈ ≈ ≈ ≈ ≈ ≈ ≈

It would be cooler if I could learn just to sit and sweat it out like Rosa. She must move, at least from one place to another, because if I am reading a magazine in the den, she is sitting by me on the couch; if I am mixing the medicine in the kitchen, she is sitting at the table. If I am in the courtyard, swatting the buzzing insects from Pepe's face, she is there perched on the iron garden chair.

I was in the living room playing Junior Scrabble with the girls when she announced like a chubby ghost from Christmas past, "You should have moved that *'cha'* over to that *'e'* to make *'hace.'* You would have gotten double points on your 'h'—but you are too far behind anyway to make a difference."

I didn't even know she was in the room. And how long had she been there to know I was that far behind?

When I went into the kitchen, she was already back there, sitting at the table telling everyone available her version of the appearance of the old Indian with the medicine. She portrayed him as a raving antichrist and assured everyone that she had just stopped me in time from administering the fatal poison to her mother.

I long to escape, to take the forty-minute ride in the jeep across the back roads to town where time is not suspended.

Where the great river *flows* rather than jumps from one crisis to the next; where cargo is loaded and unloaded; where shops open and close; where, right on the street of General San Raphael, the old decaying opera house, where no one has sung for eighty years, stands dwarfed by a ten-story modern office building as direct proof that time does not stand still.

Santa del Rio may not be the city it once was when rubber was king, but it has time. It even has a little airport which runs on its own time. The city is even catching a slight second wind as oil is being discovered in little pockets of the jungle. Outside the city, the land is divided into haciendas which are more or less immune to the economic fluctuations of the city. They are the land. They harvest the precious woods which have kept them rich for centuries and the food which has kept them self-sufficient. The haciendas here have escaped the land reforms taking place in the rest of the country because of the area's relative isolation. Saint may not be the most modern city by anyone's standards, but forty minutes by jeep from town to the hacienda is like crossing a time zone to another century.

It is cooler down in the stables. Maybe it is really not cooler there, but it doesn't smell like heat smells. The stables smell pleasantly of hay and sweat, of shadows and cool. The soft eyes of the horses are serene and protective. I would go there all the time. I would drift peacefully in the shadows and sleep, but the stables are the sanctuary of my father-in-law and I do not disturb him unless it is necessary. He is not allowed to meander around his wife's sick bed with Rosa on guard, so he stays in the stables much of the day. Sometimes we just sit there, Pepe and I, and watch the Señor soothe the great beasts with soft words and a curry comb. He does not ride, of course, now that time is suspended, just as I don't go to work and the girls don't go to school.

My father-in-law, Señor Federico Rodriguez, Senior, is in his late seventies. He is tall and lanky with a great shock of white hair and a severe limp. He always wears a little string tie no matter what the occasion. When he mounts a horse he looks like a Spanish nobleman. He looks like he is part of the horse. When he walks he looks like a man who has learned to deal with pain. His limp is worse when it is humid, and it has been very humid lately. He is a serene man and he is still calm now that the Señora is dying, but his dark eyes have become very sad.

I volunteered to get my father-in-law from the stables for dinner because I was tired of Rosa's story about her heroic anti-poison mission.

José, the stable boy, son of Ada, our housekeeper, greeted me with a guttural "ugh" and a smile. José is deaf and mute. He patted the old dog on the head and pointed me to Señor Rodriguez, who was combing down his favorite mare. I went and stood behind him for a moment. He did not turn. I did not think he heard me. I did not wish to disturb the sanctuary of the old man. I do not wish to disturb anything in the fragile balance we are living in now, but I always do.

"So someone has finally taught Pepe to heel, Rubia," he said, without turning or breaking the rhythm of his strokes.

I started. I didn't know he was aware of my presence. "No, Abuelo, the old dog is just being a pain and following me like a shadow since Abuela is so sick.... Excuse me for disturbing you but dinner is served."

"Yes," he said, still combing the mare. "I will join you at once. Thank you."

I waited in the reverie of the darkness. He dropped the brush with a start and was already past me before I realized. He was more awkward than usual with his limp so bad from the humidity. I tried not to overrun him. I tried to be close enough to speak without shouting, which only served to throw my gait off, and I tripped over poor old Pepe who was beside me as always. Even the smallest tasks have become difficult with the heat, with the tension. I wanted to tell him that Pepe was not a pain. That I was privileged that I could take care of the Señora's dog, who would have preferred, if allowed, to lie by her bed. But instead the Señor was already sitting at the table and I was late and covered in dirt.

Rosa ordered the old dog from the dining room, asked me if I had been playing in the mud, and screamed at the girls to stop giggling. She assured me with her eyes that it was my fault that the children were acting like children in the formal dining room in the house of death. My husband was barely awake. Rosa's husband, although awake, didn't care about what was going on. He is possessed by something he calls "machismo," and the care of children, especially female children, is not under his heading of machismo.

"Aren't you going to clean up?" Rosa asked me.

"Oh yes, of course," I said, wiping my hands on my pants before I strangled her. But I did not strangle her and sat down on the embroidered chair.

The girls tried not to giggle.

Señor Rodriguez toyed with the chicken and rice on his plate.

I ate.

5

T he truce which took so long to evolve may be broken but new rules have not yet been declared. Everything has become suspended. Everything has become important now that the Señora is dying.

It is important that Señor Rodriguez eat and it is important who can best persuade him to eat even though we have been stuffing him with far more food than he normally eats. It is comforting to us to think we are doing something constructive for him while the poor man is probably retching his brains out after the huge portions we coax down his throat.

It has become important to me to find out how he got his limp when I have not even thought about it for years. It sticks in my mind that if I don't find out before his wife dies that she will carry the secret with her to the grave, as if it were her limp. The first time I met Señor Rodriguez (I was holding Federico's hand down by the gate; we had not been married long), he was mounted atop a fiery stallion looking like a seventeenth century oil of a Spanish conquistador. The jungle behind him framed his straight back and impeccable dress. The limp had so shocked me when he dismounted that it made me too frightened and instantly too polite to inquire about it. It was not spoken of in the house. Once I had asked Federico when I was pregnant with my first child if there were any birth defects on his side of the family.

"I do not know what you mean," Federico had answered

indignantly.

"Your father, Federico, was he born like that?"

"If you are referring to his leg, I don't know. He was always like that as far as I can remember."

"Aren't you even curious?"

"Not anymore. I asked him once when I was a child. He was teaching me to ride and I carefully imitated his every move.

" 'My son, why do you keep mounting so awkwardly?' he asked me.

" 'It's how you do it,' I said.

" 'No, it is not. Watch more carefully this time.'

"Then I realized it was his bad leg that gave him the extra side step I was imitating when I mounted. It just shot out of my mouth:

" 'Did a horse make you crippled, Father?'

"He answered calmly, 'If you ever learn to ride better than I can, you will have my permission to call me a cripple. But not until that time.'

"I never asked again, Rubia, and I advise you to do the same. If the baby is born with a bad leg, we will name him after my father and teach him to ride well."

But I had a girl and her legs were fine. We named her after his mother and I forgot about the limp until now. Now it is on my mind all the time.

Every footstep has become important—perhaps that is why my father-in-law's limp has infiltrated my thoughts. I have the girls tiptoeing around like cherubs, even my seven-year-old, as if the sound of her little bare feet on the wooden floor could disturb the sedation of her grandmother upstairs on the other side of the house. I even use the sound of footsteps to measure the season now that it feels like the clock has stopped. The air becomes so humid, almost wet, for almost a month before the actual rainy season starts. The mornings are penetrated with a fine steam that does not burn off until the afternoon and a steamy dampness falls earlier into each evening. The paths turn to mud long before the rain starts. I listen to the sound of footsteps in the mud, and by my best calculations, the rainy season will be on us for real by the end of the month.

Hours can also be measured by the sound of footsteps coming and going to mark the passage of a visiting nurse or also our own schedule of sitting with the Señora. But these hours have nothing to do with real clocks, only with the eternity of our own crisis.

To counteract my role as high priestess of the medicine, especially after Doctor Garcia told Rosa that no, I had not been trying to poison her mother and that he had *told* me to add any drop of medicine as I saw fit, Rosa has told everyone that we are no longer to go up to visit the Señora. Instead we are on a schedule of "sitting" with her mother in an as yet indiscernible pattern. I am sure this pattern is just larger than we can imagine and after a week or so we will be able to grasp its entirety. Even Federico pulled me aside and asked me in English if I knew what the hell Rosa was doing. Sometimes it is vitally important to Rosa that one of the family be present when one of the visiting nurses is already in the Señora's room. At other times she tells us that is is not necessary that one of the family be there when there is already a nurse on duty, even if it is the same nurse we had to sit with hours before. Yesterday I had a half-hour solo sitting shift. Two days ago I sat for twelve hours with one of the nurses who slept soundly throughout most of the day, as did the Señora. I went down to the kitchen at ten in the evening when my twelve hours were up. Rosa darted her dark eyes at me and said, "Are you aware that there is no one sitting with my mother now?"

"I'm sorry," I said. "But the nurse is still there and I was just following your schedule. Let me get a cup of coffee and I'll go right back up there."

"For God's sake, Rubia," she said, "can't you leave her in

peace for a moment?"

I can't win with Rosa, at least not at her own game.

I can't even find the mysterious schedule which should give me advance notice.

"If you please, do you want me to sit with Abuela tonight, Rosa?"

"The timetable is on the refrigerator door, if you please," she said.

There are two refrigerators in the house and one freezer. I checked them all, inside and out.

"Rosa, if you please, I cannot find it there. Could you perhaps have left it somewhere else?"

"If you please, why don't you try the desk. That would seem like a logical place for it, don't you think?"

There are seven desks in the house. I had never counted them before. I checked them all.

"Rosa, if you please, it is not in any of the desks."

"Thank you for your concern, Rubia, but if you try to find out these things a little more in advance, then you would not be running around crazy at the last moment bothering everyone."

And she's right. Not about the schedule—who knows who had it last or if she hides it on purpose. But she's right; I have been running around crazy and bothering everyone lately. I don't understand why my mother-in-law is dying. I don't understand how it got so hot.

Since we are off our regular schedule and have not been able to figure out Rosa's schedule yet, and since time is suspended anyway, we just all seem to be eating most of the time which is now driving Ada into our ranks of crazy. Ada, mother of José, the stable boy, is not only the chief housekeeper here but has been the family cook for some forty years. She is a big Indian woman with more scapulars, medals, and beads around her neck than can be found in any small cathedral. When I first came here, I amused her, but after my proposal that her

son be sent to a special school for the deaf and mute, she barely
tolerates me. Her son never went to any school, but her dis-
approval of me continues. "*Dios mio,*" she says quietly and
crosses herself every time I am in her vicinity. Her only other
acknowledgment of my existence is a "Yankee" dish she con-
cocts twice a year in which she mixes baked beans, sauerkraut,
sliced potatoes, and chopped hot dogs all together and serves
like a sloppy joe over an open-faced hot dog bun.

"Why do they make these rolls this shape where you come
from, Mama?" one of my daughters will inevitably ask me every
time Ada serves this universally strange dish for which I am
careful to thank her profusely.

"I can't remember anymore," I lie.

"Perhaps it's tradition," the Señora would hopefully inter-
ject. Tradition usually covers everything here.

Ada is becoming increasingly wary of Rosa whom she had
previously adored and with whom she always discusses church
matters. Ada not only missed her day off this week, but was
severely reprimanded by Rosa for even considering leaving the
housemaid in charge of heating up food, which Ada had already
stayed up late to prepare the day before, "at a time like this."

Ada got her revenge the next morning, however, when
she served a piping hot mush of uncertain, perhaps grain,
origin. The temperature has been well over eighty each morning by the time we eat breakfast. Steam rose from the mush.

"What is this?" Rosa said.

Señor Rodriguez had already started to eat. He probably
thought he'd get a jump start before we started in with our
chorus of "you must eat something to keep your strength up."

The girls started to giggle and rolled their eyes to heaven.

Señor Rodriguez dropped his spoon and said in a loud
voice, "Yuch!"

"Girls, that is not necessary," Federico said.

"That was your father, Federico," I said.

"I said 'Yuch,' " Señor Rodriguez said.

"If you please, girls, you were told that is not necessary," Rosa said.

"That was your father both times, Rosa," I said.

"I think I can manage this myself, thank you, Rubia," Rosa said.

Rosa turned to Ada who was beaming with satisfaction and said, "Thank you for this extra appetizer, Ada, but we will be happy with just the usual eggs and rolls and iced coffee, and regular cold cereal for the children will be fine, if you please."

"I cannot do everything every day even under such emergency circumstances," Ada said firmly and quietly.

"There is no need to raise your voice," Rosa said.

Quite the contrary. It was the very calmness in Ada's voice that threw Rosa off balance. The only time Ada's voice is not usually raised is when she passes me with the sign of the cross and her delicate *"Dios mio."*

"My voice is not raised," Ada said except that it was raised and back to normal. "I cooked this because I did not have time to make the rolls this morning with so much food to prepare with so many meals we are having and some eating much more than usual," (looking at Señor Rodriguez), "and so much more food everyone is bringing to help us out," (looking at the door). "I have already had to start on the pork and rice for lunch and I have no idea yet what to have for the evening meal and no 'extra' person here to help me," she added, looking at me.

"If you please, must I do everything," Rosa said looking at me and following Ada back to the kitchen.

We ended up having an early brunch of pork and rice.

No one would play Scrabble with me in the afternoon and I was not on Rosa's sitting schedule. Federico slept after having just gotten off another long sitting shift. I wandered aimlessly muttering in English to the old yellow dog at my heels. I checked the children, mixed the medicine, walked in the garden, repotted some house plants and then saw the hot dogs defrosting in the package next to the refrigerator. Ada was still angry with Rosa and probably thought she'd swing her alliance over to the Yankee side of the family. There was no one else in the kitchen.

I cut the potatoes meticulously and dropped them by batches with a metal net into a deep pan of hot oil. I simmered a can of baked beans and added a dash of cinnamon. I steamed the sauerkraut and added an apple which I found in a cellophaned basket of fruit someone had left for the Señora. I grilled the hot dogs to perfection and switched the oven to warm. I toasted the buns lightly and set the kitchen table quietly with the most unobtrusive of dishware. The meal was to be perfect. I was only sorry that Ada didn't seem to be around anywhere to finally witness how this Yankee meal is properly prepared.

I was almost ready to call everyone to dinner when Ada and Rosa entered. They didn't seem to notice me yet. Rosa was speaking to Ada.

"What do you mean you fell asleep and haven't prepared any food for dinner?"

"But we have already had dinner," Ada said.

"That was brunch. When you have food for dinner at breakfast, it is called brunch."

"I am very tired, Señora Rosa," (until yesterday she had called her 'Rosita'), "and I have not had any time off and no one here to help me..."

They looked at me and what I was doing and stopped midstream, taking a moment to comprehend. Ada made the sign of the cross. Havoc and confusion reigned.

Had it not been for the volume of their speech, had it not been for their hands gone frenzied in the air, the hissing of their s's and the crescendos of their rolling r's, for their eyes gone wild, darting in direction but lacking in focus—had these not been, I would have ignored them as I usually do. I would not have stood there like a tourist in a foreign revolution trying to understand, trying to figure out what was going on. I would have moved. I would have remembered that Rosa is under great emotional stress—it is her mother who is dying. I would have also understood Ada's actions for she is very superstitious and the Indians here have a belief that all sickness and death is caused by another person wishing ill fate upon the ill-fated. They believe that even if a person lives to be one hundred and dies peacefully in his sleep that it was not old age that killed him but an evil wisher. They do not discount bacteria, epidemics, car accidents or lightning bolts, but hold that these things are only tools used by the ill-wisher.

"How could you do this to me," Ada screamed. "After I have taken so many years to perfect this Yankee dish for you to make it at least palatable for the rest of us. I was a fool to try to please you."

Rosa was screaming at the same time, "You just couldn't wait, could you? My mother is not even dead yet and you are taking over already. I knew it would come to this. First, you took over with the medicine and now you are taking over with the food also."

Ada gathered strength from Rosa's hysteria and continued, "I knew it was you all the time. You tried to use your evil eye on my son, watching him all the time, saying he should be sent away to a school, but God protected him and now you have gotten your eye on the Señora who is the godmother to my son."

Rosa's scream interrupted Ada. "Yes, I knew it all along but I must admit I did not expect such an open display of disrespect. Couldn't you wait until she took her last breath? She was always so kind to you. She would tell me, 'Give her time, Rosa, give her time.' But you will not even give her time to breathe her last breath."

Ada seemed to be yelling more at Rosa than at me by then. "First, she wanted to revolutionize the hacienda and educate the Indians, and then her husband, poor Federico, she embarrassed him by going into a business as if he had no money and then the business was not enough so she works this evil cancer on the godmother to my son. One year, the Señora has been in and out of the hospital!"

Rosa continued, "I will do everything in my power to stop this. I always wanted to own my own house and you even said that that would not be a bad idea. I should have known why you wanted me to move away from here, but I did not think that you would take over like this..."

The commotion brought an audience. I heard Rosa's children speaking with their father in the living room. "The Niña, the Pinta, and the Santa Maria," I used to call them when they were younger.

My girls were standing in the doorway.

Margherita ran a comb through her hair like a zombie.

Patricia stood on one bare foot, then the other. She started crying. She ran to me and clutched. I stroked the top of her long knotted curly hair.

"I knew it was her," Ada screeched at Rosa.

Ada was pulling hidden silver medals and green felt scapulars from her bosom. I heard the sound of water boiling over from the sauerkraut. I smelled the hot dogs burning. I remained semicatatonic, stroking the top of Patricia's head muttering in English, "What pretty hair my baby has."

"You are a Rodriguez only by marriage. You are Anglo, you don't belong here," Ada said.

"My mother hasn't even taken her last breath," Rosa said. "You don't belong here in her kitchen!"

Federico appeared in the doorway. "What are you talking about? My mother hates to cook. She only stepped into this kitchen to plan the daily menus. If my wife doesn't belong here in this kitchen it is only because she doesn't like to cook either!"

But I was beyond the point of understanding even the simplest facts in that foreign language by the time Federico walked in.

Margherita still stood in the doorway as I went by. Her eyes were wide and the comb led her hand through her hair. Señor Rodriguez came in through the front door and waited without speaking. I was still comforting the top of Patricia's hair. Through the hall and up the stairs, she was clutching me with frightened little bird arms so hard that I must have been carrying her but that could not have been because I don't remember my own feet on the ground, so Federico must have been dragging us both.

It never seems to bother Señor Rodriguez that nothing makes sense around here. That is his survival.

"Is it dinner time?" the Señor asked calmly.

"There will be no food tonight." Federico told him from midway up the stairs.

"Thank God," Señor Rodriguez said and walked back out the front door.

6

Federico.

I used to roll his name through my mouth and it was sustenance enough.

I was watching Federico sleep the night he so gallantly rescued me from the kitchen. It was not very interesting. I usually spend my late hours doing more enterprising things like finishing up the paper work from the store or reading a fashion magazine. But nothing is usual around here anymore except that the rest of the house was asleep and I was still awake. To clear me with the rest of civilization, many years ago I had the doctor label my wakefulness as "chronic insomnia." But I never asked for a cure—for me it is a peaceful and beautiful time and I usually make up for the lost hours of sleep during the daily afternoon siesta.

I was watching Federico sleep. I sat at the big desk overlooking the courtyard.

The house is a large two-story rectangle surrounding the inner open courtyard. Rosa and her family occupy the back of the house below some of the houseworkers' quarters. Señor and Señora Rodriguez are in one side of the house opposite to my family's quarters. The front of the house is where the kitchen, dining room and sitting rooms are. It is most spacious, especially late at night when only the long corridors connect us.

The night brings no relief from the heat. The rains will come soon. I was watching Federico sleep. His name is not so familiar in my mouth lately. I turned on the fan in the middle of the room even though it only served to move the hot air without cooling it. The drone helped to fill the quiet spaces.

I was watching Federico sleep. My love. My only love. I have enough money in the bank, my own money. Enough for the plane to take us away at any time. Enough for the girls and for Federico too if he would come. Plenty for us all to get away from this jungle next to a city named Saint. Enough to get started again somewhere, anywhere away from here. Away from this heat, this tension and even away from Federico too if need be.

My love, my only love.

We played a game when we first met. He would ask me to decide what type of day it was and I would declare it. It was that simple.

"Today is a Spanish day," I would tell him and so it would be transformed. I spoke in "baby" Spanish which delighted Federico. Slowly and patiently he taught me the phrases and the names. The trees in the park, the location of the bathroom, the state of five o'clock traffic at Columbus Circle were all suddenly seen in a different light—as if to change the symbol could change the object it represented. My name changed from Susan to Suzanna to "Rubia," which I thought had to do with a precious gem. He called me his love and it was a love I did not deem necessary to analyze; Federico was first and foremost foreign and that equaled transitory in my private vocabulary. But there was a music in his language that appealed to me, that defied five-line staffs and treble cleffs and could not be played on anything but writhing bodies on a dance floor. Federico would whisper in my ear and I will make no excuses for being so young and in love. Just as now I can offer myself no excuses for staying after so many years. It was a voluntary loss of control or at least the illusion of control.

Or I would say, "Today is an Anglo day, Federico," and

we would speak in English in the cozy vastness of New York which is a nice place to be when you are young and in love. It was something like the old Pepsi Cola ads where one group of smiling faces on the beach cuts to another group of happy faces in the park to another group of happy faces at a picnic. None coming to fruition. None seeming to mind. It was my world. It was a controlled world. It was an illusion easy to live with.

It was a feeling of power to determine the days so easily. The power had gone mad after all these many years. There is no longer any balance between the clarity of the English and the rhythm of the Latin. Federico has a belly on him now. It is not so noticeable in the right clothes, but lying there sleeping in his underwear, it hurdled the bounds of his jockey shorts. His mother is dying.

I could think of all the Anglo-Saxon words which ask such ill-fitting questions. Words like who, what, when, where, and why. Words that never fail to fill the history books and morning papers with such clear-cut answers. And how "at home" the words feel in my mouth, how gentle and pleasant, even if the answers they demand have no place here, no reality. Oh, I could see her as if she were real, sitting among the flowers in the courtyard—Federico's mother, my rival, my mentor, my alter-ego from the old world. I could picture her from my window overlooking the courtyard with her long black hair falling with the darkness that shone. She must have been as beautiful when she was young as she was when she was old and still well. I could see her in the courtyard sitting among the roses.

The roses. She would wander among the roses, touching them, sighing deep sighs, chattering in sudden, soft-spoken outbursts punctuated by long silences. She would sit upon the rusting wrought-iron garden chair and sip an iced tea. The roses have survived all odds and not by tediously weeding hands, temperature controls, or carefully monitored soil content. The rain would come each year and swallow them mid-blossom, but they would return again the next year to her touch, to her sighs. They are not your long-stemmed, hot house beauties. They are small clusters of pale pinks and deep reds which rival the sturdy philodendron and crayola hibiscus only by their subtlety.

"Something from the old country, these roses, something to have pride in," she would tell me as if they were actual buds imported by her forefathers one hundred fifty years ago. A hundred and fifty years! And they were still arguing, the Señor and Señora Rodriguez, over which place in Spain was better to have come from. They spoke of their roots like tourists on visa. The Señora was careful to impress upon me that their blood was pure—"from Spain." That there was no Indian blood in their veins, while Señor Rodriguez's cheekbones are so high that they almost sit in his long narrow eyes and his skin is dark and dry below his white hair. That there was no black blood in their veins, while my husband, whom I am told favors the Señora's parents, has very curly hair and skin the color of milk chocolate.

Yet the Señora effected her prejudices with grace. She would ask me to tell her about the United States. She would ask me to tell her about what it was like to grow up in New York, and when I would return from a visit, it was to her that I reported. She would say with a sigh, "Ah yes, I will modernize this place to fit in with the rest of the world. Someday." She could have travelled around the world a thousand times, yet she rarely made a trip into town. She never even once visited my shop where her white lace gowns were made to order. But she never failed to ask me for business reports: insurance premiums, contracts, robe designs, bra fasteners, down to the last penny. She never interfered, yet she was always in control. She was not always kind to me. I was not always kind to her. I am an obstinate student. And as I imagined her in the garden, her grace was as formidable as ever, her skin dark against the white gown and her black hair loose and flowing. Among the roses which have survived all odds.

I was overcome by the slow passage of night in the house of death. I longed to touch my imaginings as flesh and reassure myself that I was not invisible in this strange land. I lifted my hand towards the vision. It waved back. I lifted my hand again. It waved back again. I have never believed in ghosts but...

"She is dead," I screamed, "Federico, she is dead. I see her ghost in the garden."

"Stop screaming," he woke up screaming. "Were you with her when it happened? Did you call the doctor? Stop screaming. This is no way to announce my mother's death to the family. Be quiet at least for the sake of my father. Is there still time to kiss her hand?"

Kiss her hand? She was dead in the courtyard.

In the courtyard?

There were people in the hall. Federico in his jockey shorts. The Señor calmly evoking the gods. Ada with rosary beads. The girls in the doorway giggling with frightened eyes. Rosa screaming that she told me so. Footsteps came from everywhere, down the stairs, in the hall, up the stairs to the room of death. I thought the skies would surely open up. Saints scurried past the old Indian man on foot. And horses, I could hear them everywhere with their nostrils dilated and their manes on fire. Before I reached the room, Rosa had already visited it and was back out in the hall screaming at me, "Again! Again, you could not wait until she takes her last breath."

I could no longer stand for such shit. "This is no way to talk now, Rosa, we must stand together as a family."

I moved to embrace her. She grabbed my outstretched arm and pulled me into the room where Señora Rodriguez was sedately sleeping. Yes, sleeping. I could see her breathing through her open mouth and her chest moving ever so slightly.

The visiting nurse with sleep bulging from her eyes assured me in cool professional tones that the patient had been sleeping comfortably all night. I was put through a brief interrogation. I was to be arrested certainly. Only Señor Rodriguez's eyes were kind. By general consensus, it was agreed that I was in need of sedation. I refused. Rosa refused me permission to make sure the girls were all right downstairs. She would handle it herself, she said. If only her brother could take care of me, she said.

In the big bed, facing the windows overlooking the courtyard, Federico put his arms around me tightly as if to force me into sleep.

7

T he gray morning sun struggles through the thick
haze towards the window. It will be months before
it shines through. It only replaces the darkness
with pale mist. And more heat.

Rosa, according to her mysterious schedule, has ended
the night sitting shifts for the family so Federico gets to sleep
at night. He tries not to sing in the morning now that his mother
is dying but he can't help himself. So he sings in English now,
not to break the mood of the house, the heaviness of which is
Spanish. His accent is thick.

The door was open to the bathroom. The smell of shaving
lotion moved heavily on the steam from his shower. He was
doing a fair job of lead vocal on "To Love Somebody." I woke
up against my wishes.

He sat on the edge of the bed with a towel wrapped around
his middle and put his socks on. I put my arms around his
waist. If I could pull him back down again in bed and he were
sleeping again then I would not have to get up. He pulled away
from my arms.

"You're getting fat, Federico."

"No, my muscles are getting large only. Now get up."

"No, you must let me sleep for a little longer. I'll eat later.
I don't think I can face them this early anyway."

He switched to Spanish. "I am serious now. It is time to

get up."

"Why?"

"Why? Because you have work to do."

I switched to Spanish also. "And what is that?"

"You are going to work today, if you please."

"You are crazy."

"No, I am not."

"You want me to get into more trouble than I already am in this house. Rosa would be bubbling with my lack of respect. She would even be angry at you."

"I don't care, Rubia. It will be good for you. You need a change of scenery. You are not normally one to be having visions."

"I am too exhausted."

"Get up. I'll drive you into the city myself."

Rosa was fuming when she saw me dressed for work. She surveyed my purse on the table in the hallway with a cluck of her tongue. Federico told José to bring the jeep around.

"At least *I* will be here," Rosa said to no one in particular.

The children were given cereal and milk. Mystery mush was placed before all the adults except me. I was getting nervous. If they were getting mush, what would I be given? I envisioned burnt mush. I envisioned cold burnt hot dogs. The children ate. Señor Rodriguez ate. Rosa's husband left the table with a grunt. Ada, beaming, brought in a separate tray with my breakfast. There was fresh fruit in a bowl, iced coffee in a chilled glass. A fresh baked roll sat beside an egg, sunny side up, and four strips of bacon. I was confused. My forehead broke out in a sweat.

"Can I have a piece of your bacon, Mama?" Patricia asked.

"Of course, dear." My hand shook as I passed it to her.

Ada came back out from the kitchen with a single white rose in a slender crystal vase.

"Oh, I almost forgot this," she said casually placing the rose along side my plate.

"Oh, my God," Rosa said, "you have gone crazy too along with Rubia."

Ada had been waiting for an opener. She stood behind me and placed one hand gently on my shoulder. "You must show more respect, Señora Rosa, to those God has chosen to see his saints."

"You have gone out of your mind. My mother is not yet a saint."

Ada had her where she wanted. "So you do not think your mother is a holy woman! She was a saint while she was alive and she will be a saint when she is dead. We must not question the ways of God," squeezing my shoulder, "who sometimes works in mysterious ways."

She went back to the kitchen.

"Can I have another piece of bacon, Mama?"

"Of course, Sweetheart."

The gray air was thick with heat. A jeep over back roads, some of them only dirt in places and already soggy from the rain that will not come, is no place for intimate conversation. There was a large towel over my seat to protect my dress. I didn't remember having put it there as I have on other mornings. We had almost to shout to hear one another over the engine.

"How do you feel?" Federico asked.

"Oh, I don't know. It seems strange to be going to work as if it was just another normal day."

"It is a normal day."

"Sure, that's why you are so concerned to get me out of the house today, because it is a normal day, and last night, was a normal night too, I suppose."

"I am so concerned to get you 'out of the house,' as you say, so you will have a normal day and maybe we can all have a normal night tonight."

"Well, I hope you are right."

"I am right. I have faith in you. Just try not to think about anything, ANYTHING, except the shop today."

"But I am already thinking about it. Maybe it is better that I talk about it."

"You are going to talk about it?"

"Yes, I have to get it out of my system."

"Don't you think that's carrying it a little too far?"

"What do you want me to do, pretend like it never happened?"

"That would be just fine."

"Oh, so I should just close my eyes tightly and it'll go away."

"Well, you kept your eyes open last night and it appeared. Why shouldn't it go away if you close them today?"

"Federico, whether it was a vision or an apparition, it happened."

"And what may I ask is the difference between a vision and an apparition?"

"Damn it, that's not what I meant. I just want to talk about it, that's all."

"Well, it would be better if you didn't. You know how superstitious the Indians are. Ada will have the news all over the hacienda. Let's keep the news out of town if we can help it. Don't tell me that your herd of Marias never gossip. People would be pointing fingers at you in the street. Don't you think my mother deserves a little more peace than that?"

"What are you talking about now? I am not talking about talking about my experience in the street. I am talking about talking about it right now with you."

"Well, go ahead then, talk."

The image came back slowly.

"Well, are you going to talk?"

"I'm thinking."

"Oh, you want to think about it."

"No, I want to talk about it. I just want to make it real for you...the way her dark hair was so long."

"Her hair is long."

"I know, but the way it flowed past her back so real, and the gown she wore was so white and long. It was so white it was almost shining."

"Rubia, she always wears white gowns. You get them for her yourself at the store."

"And the roses, Federico, it seems so dull to describe them this morning. They were so bright last night and they were all in bloom."

"Rubia, the roses are all in bloom."

"Then everything I saw must have been real. Is that what you mean by your little remarks?"

"I'm sorry, Rubia. I am not trying to be sarcastic. I just mean that things were just as they are and that you were tired and under much tension and Rosa and Ada had just unleashed all their tensions on you for trying to help out in the kitchen and you couldn't sleep and you were thinking so hard about my mother that you imagined you saw her in the garden. That's all I meant."

"I wasn't thinking about your mother until I saw her there, Federico. I was thinking about us, when we first met in New York and how simple and clear everything was in English."

"And do you think if we switched this conversation from Spanish to English right now that things would be clearer?"

"No. No, I understand that nothing is that simple. I was just trying to tell you what I was thinking of before I saw her in the garden. It was all so real!"

"You know that it would be impossible for my mother to be in the garden."

"Yes, I know that. She has to be carried to sit in the chair for a few hours."

"You understand that in English too?"

"Cut the shit."

"I mean do you understand that inside, deep down?"

"Yes. Maybe we are speaking different languages though. Do you ever think in English anymore? I have been a lot lately."

"No, not really. Except for sometimes when I am speaking to you and I don't understand what you are saying so I try to think it through in English."

"Even if I am speaking in Spanish?"

"More so if you are speaking in Spanish."

Federico opened the door for me and drove away. I thought it would be different when I went back to the shop. It had only been two weeks or not quite since I had been there, but I thought it would be different. Instead it was like reentering Planet Normalcy and everything, even the heat, which had seemed so real and so intense at the hacienda, now felt like a distant abstraction, like I had had a touch of the flu or something.

The first customer of the day was Señora Gonsalves. I programmed myself on automatic and tried to go through the motions. The shop bell tinkled when she opened the door. The sound of carpeted footsteps. The simplicity of buying and selling.

Señora Gonsalves is what is known in this business as a connoisseur. She does not need to buy a bra to hold up her breasts—a dainty 34A, nor does she buy underpants—a size five and always bikini—to pull up a sagging bottom or to tuck in a tummy. She buys underwear because she likes its feel against her skin. The finer the lace, the silkier the fabric, the greater the emphasis on design and the less on confinement, the better she likes it. The connoisseurs are few and far between, plumper women are more in vogue here. She buys when she is happy and she is happy most of the time.

"How is your mother-in-law, Rubia?"

"She is, I'm afraid, about the same. Yet she doesn't seem to be in any pain at the present time by the grace of God and the medication the doctor has prescribed."

People must be tired of asking me how she is. She has been in and out of the hospital for a year now. I don't think they understand behind my set answers that she is not just sick this time, but dying.

I continued. "It is in the hands of God. Please say a prayer for her, if you will, Señora."

I kept going through the motions. And besides, what has death to do with plush carpet beneath one's high heels, lace against one's tits, silk beneath one's crotch?

I smiled. It was easier at the store.

". . . and Federico, as handsome as always, I hope."

"You would not say that if you saw him in the morning before I come to work!"

I was lying, of course. The bastard. He is vibrant in the morning, singing in the mirror, smiling, no matter how gray the sky is, no matter how hot it is, but I was not there to sell him to her.

". . . and your husband?"

"Oh very well." She blushed. She has been married for five years and she is still blushing.

She looked around to see if anyone was within earshot and then leaned over the glass display counter to my ear as if she were about to deliver a hot piece of gossip about someone else. "We are thinking of having another baby."

"You are here for a black negligee then?"

She blushed again and laughed. "My, Rubia, nothing so drastic as to shock him into impotence!"

"Ah, then vibrant pink, silk maybe. Pink for a girl this time after already having two sons."

"But they are such fine boys and such good luck having them—my last labor was a breeze."

"Ice blue then and shimmering."

"Blue for a boy if I read your thoughts. No. No. Just another healthy baby will be fine. Boy or girl is really of no importance to me. Anyway, I just came for a strapless slip for a new dress."

"Well, then something neutral—a beige lace gown with a swirl on the bottom. I have just the right thing. One of our own designs."

Just the "right thing" with a matching robe and a strapless slip later, Señora Gonsalves left, still blushing.

I went through the motions and the motions finally began to take over.

There is an insanity at the shop which excludes all others. And there are no ghosts there, either of the dead or of the not yet dead. Nothing is of real importance or necessity there. The colors glimmer and delight. The fabrics feel soft in your hands. Everything carries a brand of the unreal like an old-fashioned confectioners shop but with the whisper of intimacy.

There are seven Marias employed at "Rubia's" not including Maria-Elena, my assistant manager.

"Makes it easy for you, Rubia," one of the Marias on the front counter will say. "All there is for you to remember are the ones not named Maria." Which should leave me only my own name to remember since there is no one else there not named Maria at present. Federico thinks is is some type of employment criterion I've established. But it is only another brand of the unreal that is there. And it is not my fault that the majority of the female population in the city is named Maria. It almost makes sense that in a town named Saint, the women should all be named Maria.

But it is not as easy as the Maria who always tells me how easy it is for me says.

Maria-Elena is easy because she is called always "Maria-Elena," although she tries my patience in other ways. The god who handed out business acumen was awake and alert the day she was born, but the god who hands out self-confidence was surely in a coma.

It is the other seven Marias' names which make my life at the shop difficult. There is not one of them who somehow does not have an uncanny sense of identity. No matter how many times I call out "Maria," which is naturally a good many times during the selling day, the Maria I am thinking of answers. I have played a thousand little games since accumulating so many Marias. I will call out "Maria," thinking of the Maria on the other side of the store who is busy with a customer when there are several other Marias right near me who are not busy. Sure enough, the Maria across the shop will answer. I make eye contact with one Maria and call softly for another Maria not in eyesight and the right Maria answers. I will think of no particular Maria at all and call Maria, and no one will answer. "Maria," I will say again, thinking of all the Marias and they all answer. Even the ones sewing on the machines in back will call out to ask me what I want.

It would be easier if they had different names.

I plead with them, "But how did you know it was you I wanted?"

They answer, "You called my name didn't you?"

"Yes, but your names are all the same."

They have heard this before.

"Look, you wanted me and so you called for me and here I am."

The three Marias in the back on the lace machines are the scariest of all. Perhaps they are extra-terrestrial. They came with the shop. Or rather, before the shop was, they were.

I wanted to work outside the house because I was bored and because my past project, trying to propel the hacienda into the twentieth century, had failed. Having a "boutique" was in the back of my mind because that was the rage back home. I knew the location was perfect the second I saw the "For Sale" sign in the window of "Isabella's Fine Lace and

Linen" shop. I knew Isabella casually and knew for a fact that
the only reason she was going out of business was because
everyone in Saint who was ever going to have fine lace and
linen already had enough of it for the next three generations.
I chose to convert it into a lingerie boutique because the only
thing I ever sold in my life, aside from a summer selling ice
cream at Oakland Beach which made me nauseous by mid-
July, was lingerie. I sold bras and girdles in Macy's part-time
through college.

The three Marias who made lace in the back room for
Isabella's Fine Lace and Linen shop continued to make lace
after Isabella was long gone. They continued to make lace after
I had signed the papers and promenaded into what I thought
was a vacant store. There the three Marias continued to make
lace in the backroom as I directed the workmen where to lay
the carpeting, where to make the partitions, where to place
the chrome and glass counters. There the three Marias continued to make lace as stock was arranged and grand opening day
approached with fresh cut flowers in the windows.

"Why are you in such a panic?" Federico asked. "Why
don't you just tell them to leave?"

"Don't you understand?" I screeched. "Am I talking to
myself when I speak to you? I have told them to leave. Every
day I tell them. They tell me not to worry about it. Then I ask
them if they understand what I'm telling them—that this is no
longer 'Isabella's Fine Lace and Linen.' I tell them that this
is my bra and girdle store and they tell me that it is of no
importance. My store is opening tomorrow and there are three
ancient gray-haired spiders in my backroom weaving lace."

"You want me to ask them to go then? You want me to go
down there and get them out after you told me this was your
project and I was to let you sink or swim on your own?"

"Yes! That is exactly what I want you to do."

Federico went down to Saint begrudgingly. But I was

grateful just the same.

He came back looking very confused.

"Well, what happened?"

"They told me not to worry."

I shrieked.

"But don't worry, I spoke to Juan Guernica and you can have them arrested for trespassing."

"Didn't he also tell you that I had already spoken with him. Shit, Federico, I can't have three old women arrested. That would not only be cruel, it would be lousy publicity for the store on opening day."

"Well, don't press charges after the police get them out. Maybe that will be all they need to make them understand."

"No, it won't work. I couldn't do it and they would come back the next day anyway."

"It'll work out, Rubia. I know. They will understand when the shop opens or at least they will understand the next week when they don't receive a paycheck."

"Don't you understand," I said to the three Marias. "You have been here in my store for two weeks now and I have not paid you."

"Don't worry. Business will pick up," one Maria said.

"It is of no importance," said another Maria.

"We are not worried," still another said.

And they were not, not one of them, worried. They were as ancient then as they are now. They have not aged in the eight years since I have had the shop because it would be impossible to look any older than they already did.

I thought of them as elves in the fairy tale about the impoverished cobbler and thought—if only this were a shoe store. Except that if it had been a shoe store, these elves would still be making lace.

All three elves are plump. One complains constantly about corns, bunions and callouses on her feet, although I rarely see her in any position except sitting. Another wears a hair net woven with tiny sparkles over a few strands of gray hair. The third chain smokes little cigars. All three continued to make lace without pay for six months until I got tired of looking at them and the bolts of spider webs. I began to have fantasies of sabotaging their machines. I had dreams of finding them rigor-mortisized in the same spinning positions before I went through with my plans for sabotaging their machines. Then, in desperation, I, who had never designed anything and had only started sewing under Señora Rodriguez's watchful eye, began designing simple gowns and robes to use up the damn lace. They received their back pay. I pay them an incredibly high salary today. They have made me a rich woman. I have an exclusive line which was featured in the New York Designers Review for the first time three years ago. Their lace now covers some pretty famous tits and asses.

8

≈ ≈ ≈ ≈ ≈ ≈ ≈ ≈ ≈ ≈ ≈

Rosa had declared a state of emergency while I was at work. She had the visiting nurse in an uproar, supervising and criticizing her nursing ability, while Señor Rodriguez, whose turn it was to sit, sat patiently by. Rosa then called the parish priest in for last rites for her mother even though there was no change in the Señora's condition. She told every ear available that I was nothing more than a "Yankee materialist" for leaving her to run the house and take care of her mother "by herself." Rosa apparently didn't notice the rest of the family, the visiting nurse service, three housemaids and Ada, who were also there at the time. Nor did she remember that I was allowed to do little more than mix the medicine after supper when I was home. In fact, the medicine did not even have to be mixed on a daily basis; I only did so to adjust the dosage and to have something to do.

"Why didn't you warn me?" I asked Federico after I had stepped from the steamy afternoon heat into the screaming frenzy.

"I didn't know. I was in town on business."

But before I could pursue this, Rosa continued, "I cannot manage this entire household by myself, Rubia. My mother will have to be put back in the hospital and it's your fault. Unless, of course, you plan on giving up your job, which is not necessary anyway, for the sake of my mother."

I had no intentions of returning to work on a regular basis

while the Señora was still sick, but I did not like it being put to me in such a manner.

"I am not giving up my business, Rosa. Nor do I have any intention of letting you put your mother in the hospital against her wishes."

"You are only jealous," Ada said to Rosa. "You told me yourself that if your mother was going to appear to anyone that she would have appeared to you. You must learn not to question the ways of God."

"Jealous! This has nothing to do with Rubia's hallucinations or the fact that she is insane."

"Fuck off," I told her calmly in English, surprising myself that I had reverted back to English after having spent the day at the shop thinking and doing solely in Spanish.

"Ease up, Rubia," Federico said in English.

The argument did ease up during dinner because of the children. But it continued afterwards at the family conference Rosa had called, at which time Doctor Garcia, at Rosa's urgent request, joined us. Ada served brandy around the table. Not one for small talk when he was called away from his after-dinner chess game, over a patient who should have died long ago, Doctor Garcia took a sip of brandy and got right to the point:

"Now why do you think your mother should be put back in the hospital, Rosa? There is no change in your mother's condition. I spoke to the nurse after you called this afternoon."

Rosa then gave a detailed account of my hallucination of the previous night and a minute-by-minute "summary," she called it, of her harrowing day taking care of her mother "by myself."

"It was only jealousy," Ada said as she refilled Doctor Garcia's brandy glass. "She told me last week that she wished Rubia was back at work and not bothering everyone here and today she said that her mother should have appeared to her instead."

"Rubia's insanity is only a coincidence to the question of my mother going into the hospital for better care! And you were not invited to this discussion and may be excused, if you please."

"Rubia," Doctor Garcia said as Ada took Rosa's glass away. "As your name has been mentioned frequently in this discussion, do you have anything to say?"

"Yes. As you know, my sister-in-law was not 'alone' in the care of her mother today and I do not think it is merely a coincidence, Doctor, that this whole change of attitude has come about since my vision of last night.

"My mother-in-law requested that if there was nothing more to be done that she be able to die at home where she is comfortable and where her suffering would not be prolonged needlessly. Her wish has been respected thus far and it only seems to be after last night that anyone is questioning it. I don't think it should bring about any change in her request. It is me who had the vision, not her, so why should it necessitate a change in her request. If anyone should have to go to the hospital because of last night, it should be me. Ha, ha!"

Except that no one else laughed. Rosa's husband even had the nerve to issue a "that wouldn't be such a bad idea" eyebrow raise.

"Federico?" I asked.

Silence.

"Doctor?"

"I think a checkup at the office would suffice, Rubia. I'll prescribe some tranquilizers now and a sleeping pill, and perhaps a referral to one of my colleagues who is more adept at handling cases of this nature would be in order."

Federico said, "Doctor, if you please, just to clear this matter up, is there anything more the hospital would be doing for her than we are doing here?"

"No. no. I think this is only a stress-related illness and I think it will pass with the tranquilizers and with time."

It took a long silent minute to grasp the learned doctor's words. Finally, Señor Rodriguez said, "With all respect, Doctor, I think my son's question refers to *my* wife's condition."

Ada had placed a fruit and cheese board in front of him. He did not eat.

"Yes, excuse me, of course," the doctor said. "No, the care the Señora is receiving here is very good. It is as good or better than any hospital can give. She would be perhaps on continuous IV fluids at the hospital instead of the two or three a week, under the doctor's supervision, given here. But the medicine that Rubia makes for her would be the same and the general regimen would be the same. Besides, she is doing much better than anyone expected and she is still taking pureed food and is doing very well with her fluid intake by mouth. She even had enough strength to try to get out of bed by herself two or three times last week. The nurse had to use restraints."

"Well, it is settled," Señor Rodriguez said.

"Rosa?" Doctor Garcia said.

"Well, it goes without saying that I also want my mother's wishes carried out, although she wouldn't be aware of a change at this point. It is not my mother's fault that everyone was in a state of hysteria for over an hour at 2:00 A.M. last night. Nor is it my mother's fault that Rubia left her children here all day to go and sell bras and girdles which somehow also necessitated that her husband be in town all day away from his mother's bedside. No, it is not her fault that the workings of this entire house were left solely to me with the little sleep I was allowed."

"Rosa! I did not leave my children here. This is where they live. This is their home!"

"And I was in town today not on the whim of my wife, but to tend to business there which concerns the running of this house which I was no longer able to postpone," Federico said.

I switched to English because I couldn't help myself. "She really pisses me off, using her mother's dying request as a threat."

"Rubia!" Federico said.

I switched back to Spanish. "You had to run this *whole* house by yourself for a *whole* day not to mention the assistance you received from a private duty nurse, three maids, Ada, your father, and your husband. For that matter, why didn't you get your husband to help you if your day was so tough."

"Rubia," Federico said.

Señor Rodriguez chuckled and finally ate a piece of cheese.

Rosa's husband gave Rosa a disgusted look and left the table.

"Excuse me, if we are finished, I will be leaving also," Doctor Garcia said.

"But nothing is decided yet," Rosa said.

"Nothing is decided? Well, if nothing is still decided, why don't we go right to the source and ask your mother what she prefers to do?"

"Oh my God," Rosa wailed. "You are so disrespectful to my mother!"

"Well, if you can't decide, Rosa, let her decide. We should have thought of this to begin with."

Doctor Garcia opened his mouth only to be cut short by Rosa again. "Oh, you are terrible to say such a thing. But go ahead, Rubia, ask the doctor. He said they opened her up and closed her. Isn't that what you said, Doctor? He said the cancer was everywhere, didn't you, Doctor? He said that she was terminally ill, didn't you, Doctor?"

"So what," I said. "That doesn't mean that she no longer understands what is happening to her. She can still give us an answer."

"Rubia, you have said enough. Why do you show such

disrespect to my mother when she can no longer speak or understand."

"Rosa..." the doctor said.

"Rosa," I said. "You are crazy. You mean you no longer talk to her or let her answer when you sit with her for hours? You treat her like a vegetable?"

"You not only have hallucinations, but you are hearing things too, now. And what may I ask does my poor mother say to you in your dreams?"

"Rosa..." Doctor Garcia said.

"Please, Rubia, please," Federico said.

"Doctor," I said, "please tell her that her mother can understand and speak or I give you my permission in front of everyone here to commit me to the hospital right now!"

"Rosa..." the doctor said.

"Do you forget that I was with you last night; we were all with you last night in the room. You didn't speak to her then, did you? And she did not answer did she?"

"She was sleeping, Rosa. I would not disturb her when she is sleeping."

"Oh, so now you admit she was sleeping and not appearing to you in the garden."

"Rosa," Doctor Garcia said and finally went right ahead. "Your mother *is* able to speak and to understand. Some days she can only nod but even then her nods are coherent to the questions. You must be aware of that. At least the nurses told you that, didn't they?"

"*I* told the nurses that she was delirious and could not make sense," Rosa answered.

"And the rest of you? Federico? Señor Rodriguez? She doesn't speak to you either?"

"She has never spoken to me," Federico said.

"She doesn't speak to me either," Señor Rodriguez said. "But I don't speak to her either. I pray only."

"Well, Doctor, thank you for your time," Rosa said. "I think it is important that we do not tire our mother by having her make important decisions when she is so ill. She will stay here, of course. Good night."

"Good night."

"Good night."

Rosa placed one of the tranquilizers that Doctor Garcia left for me with a glass of water and said, "You will take one of these three times a day, Rubia. Is that clear?"

It was clear. I took it.

Rosa continued as she walked back to the kitchen "... well, at least now I know why my mother looks so worn after the Rubia sits with her because the Rubia chatters to her and asks her too many questions."

"Federico, why didn't you tell me you were going to stay in town all day. I would have come back here earlier to help out."

"Because I didn't know till I got there and anyway how could I tell you? You slept all the way home in the car."

"Papa, will you come and take Mama for us," I heard Margherita say. "Vacation is over tomorrow, so we all have to get up early for school in the morning."

"Well, tell her to come here, Margherita."

"I can't. She fell asleep playing Scrabble with us and the stupid dog keeps farting."

"You shouldn't use that language."

"Mama does."

He took me out of the room and the old dog followed. I was not really asleep. I just couldn't wake up from the tranquilizer.

"You want to make love to me, is that why you are carrying me, Federico?"

"Why do you say such things, Rubia?"

He put me on the bed and took my shoes off.

"Why not, my love, it has been a long time."

"Because my mother is dying right across the courtyard from us."

"But we are not in her room, are we?"

"Christ, maybe you should take the sleeping pill as well as the tranquilizer, and why do you always curse in English at Rosa?"

"All right, I'll curse at her in Spanish."

"Just leave it alone."

"OK. As long as you don't leave me alone."

"Rubia, we are not making love."

"All right. All right. Let's go do it in the kitchen then if we can't here."

"You are crazy from the tranquilizer, Rubia. And besides the dog is staring."

He was right. Pepe was staring. I stared back at him until I fell asleep.

9

The bed felt oppressively warm after so many hours of sleep and dreams of roses growing into monsters which chased me through the garden. It felt like one of the monster roses had also stepped on my head during the night. I took my morning tranquilizer without prompting to kill the pain.

I was first down to breakfast for a change. Ada was gravely disappointed that my night passed without incident. She refused to believe that a dream about roses, even monster roses, didn't have some deeper significance that I refused to see. I finally convinced her that the dream was drug-induced and she decided that God doesn't work with people who take drugs.

The girls came down to breakfast with their school uniforms on. So they *had been* on vacation and not staying home because the Señora is dying. They looked precious in the blue and white seersucker jumpers with the Sacred Virgin of the Rosary insignia. But something about these uniforms on my children always makes me nervous. I know the school teaches my children well and I know my children are learning under the steady gaze of the black-habited nuns because I go over their homework with them. I also know they are doing well because the nuns tell me so at the parent-teacher meetings. But I do not know what grade they are in. I will never admit my fear that the nuns do this on purpose to keep them there forever until they come out as nuns also. I ask the nuns the same question each time, casually of course, just slipping it into the conversation—"and what year are they in now, Sister?" And they smile at me benevolently and ask what I am talking about. Perhaps the information is unknown or marked classified by the Sacred Virgin of the Rosary herself.

Señor Rodriguez said that he was happy to see me down before the rest and called me aside to ask if there were any incidents during the night that he should know about.

"Well, Rubia?" Rosa said when she swished down the stairs to take her place on the kitchen chair where she sat and sweated all day.

"Well what?"

"Well, any news from the other side?"

"We are on the same side," I answered knowing full well what she meant. Although she did appear to have changed sides during the night, having retired her basic curtain-flowered dress for a basic black.

I was trying to coax Patricia's long curls through a comb and into braids when Federico came down and looked at me as if he had never seen this battle before.

"Mama, please don't cut it."

"What are you talking about? Does this look like a comb or a scissors?"

Margherita laughed as her own hand moved easily through her constantly combed hair. "Aunt Rosa told her that you would have to cut her hair off if she didn't start combing it herself."

"I never said that, Patricia. By the way, what grade are you going to be in now, Margherita? And, Patricia, what grade will you be in?"

"Mama," Margherita said. "You know this is just the first day back after vacation. This is not the beginning of a new year."

"How can you tell?"

"Because we know."

"Well, what grade are you still in then?"

"Rubia, they attend a convent school and not a New York City public school," said Rosa, implying that my own education in the New York public school system was sorely lacking.

"Thank you, I know they attend a convent school, Rosa. That is exactly why I am so concerned about what grade they are in."

Patricia let out a little squeal when I caught a knot in the comb and Federico asked what the hell I was doing. Maybe it was too torturous for a little girl so I settled for a pony tail with a few knots left in it.

"Rubia, I asked you what are you doing?"

"Well, isn't a pony tail better?"

"What are you all dressed up for?"

"I'm not all dressed up. I am dressed for work."

"Why are you going to work today?"

"Didn't you insist yesterday?"

"That was yesterday. You never go to work today."

It was true. It was Wednesday and I usually took the day off and had Maria-Elena open and close the store on Wednesday. I don't like to work straight through the week if I can help it.

"Well, I figure the same principle applies today and it will be good for me to get out of the house."

"You're going to make a habit of it? You're even going to work on your day off?"

"What?"

"What about the medicine for my mother?"

"You sound like your sister. You know I make the medicine after dinner."

"What about what the doctor said? He said you needed rest and an environment free from stress."

"Exactly why I'm going. I couldn't have said it better myself."

"Did you take your tranquilizer this morning?"

"Yes, I did."

"Well, then you can't drive."

"You usually go into town today. Can't you drop me off?"

"I am not going today."

"Well, then I'll have somebody else drive me."

"Well, I'll have to drive you then if you insist."

I don't understand anything anymore. I have a lot to learn from Señor Rodriguez about not letting that bother me.

Federico was fuming as he drove me down. I figured that he was upset because I wasn't sticking around the house to help Rosa so I asked him if we could go back early so we could both stick around the house to help Rosa.

"When I come to pick you up is when I come," he replied.

"Fuck you," I said in English.

"You will never be a lady with your mouth," he answered in Spanish.

I have set up the shop to run without my presence; it is not my life. I do not know what my life is. Some weeks I am gone for a fashion review. Sometimes I don't feel like working. Other weeks, I spend twelve hours a day there and then bring my work home with me at night. On the average I spend four days a week at the store at least for part of the day. I am proud of the way my business runs.

It felt good to be back again, amid the quiet chatter and the air-conditioning set a little too cool, even if my presence was not necessary. I was feeling a little sentimental perhaps from the tranquilizer. I felt proud of Maria-Elena even though she seemed wary of my arrival on a Wednesday. She was hired as extra part-time help four years ago wearing dime-store underwear. Now she wears Lily of France and handles the store smoothly with a keen sense of organization and a pretty profit margin. I have tried to promote her from assistant manager to manager many times, for that is in fact what she is now. Her constant refusal to be promoted gets on my nerves, especially now that I spend more and more time on promotion and design of my own line. She tells me that she is not worthy.

I was glad I went to work on a day I wasn't expected. I did not wish to be bothered with any supervisory decisions that Maria-Elena usually handles on a Wednesday. I wished only to tread plush carpet, mingle with the crowd and sell bras. The respectful hush of the day before had worn off. All the Marias were treating me normally except for Maria-Elena who had turned her respectful hush into aggressive helpfulness. She was determined to destroy my escapism. Her tiptoeing on the carpet drove me crazy. She kept jumping in while I was trying to work, telling me to sit down, telling me she'd take this customer, telling me how exhausted I must have been. She found me on the stock ladder in the back looking for pink underpants for Señora Baptista. "You could at least let me get the stock for you, Rubia."

"Maria-Elena, thank you, but I'm not the one who's sick in my house. I'm all right."

She breathed a deep sigh. We have always liked each other. We have always worked well together. But somehow I am always in a state of blasphemy in her eyes.

I was sure my morning would improve when Señora Cortez, with her two daughters, daughter-in-law, and niece, paraded through the front door like a queen with entourage. She was about to hold court. I always expect her to snap her fingers and call "waiter." And if she ever did, I would still come running. I would still wait on her hand and foot. She is my baby and I have fallen over many a customer and many a counter to wait on her promptly and personally. Maria-Elena told me once how she had come in last year while I was away and after ceremoniously feeling a few lace gowns between her fingers, she announced to the four Marias and Maria-Elena humbly at her heels and asking if they could help her, that she would be back when the Rubia was here.

"She never even asked if you were here. Nor did she ask when you'd be back when you didn't suddenly appear," Maria-Elena told me. "She just threw her head over her shoulder, made her announcement and walked out."

Six years ago, Señora Cortez had a mastectomy and made it no secret. I fitted her prosthesis, a fact which she also made known. It was the first prosthesis I fitted and not into one of those plain pre-ordered pocket bras, but into a delicate design of our own lace.

In her daily clothes, which she has not modified, it is impossible to tell which breast has been removed. That has endeared my efforts at corsetry with the female community. She will, when asked, answer, "Oh yes, I'll tell you all about it." And begins, "When I had my breast removed, it was my right one, of course." And then she casually looks down at her chest and says, "No, it was my left one, of course. No, no, the right." Still looking down, she says with a sigh, "Well, I can't remember which one right now, but that is not important, is it?"

Even I succumbed to her game for a while, until I remembered "M" for mastectomy and "M" for marriage—one wears one's wedding ring on the left side.

As always, Señora Cortez had a list meticulously written on embossed stationery. The ritual began as she removed it from her leather purse with her carefully manicured hands.

"May I be of any service to you, Señora Cortez, or to any one of your lovely family?"

"Yes. But first, Rubia, you must tell me how I can be of service to you and your family."

"Señora, you have already been most gracious with your flowers and fruit, which we are most thankful for."

"But these are only orchids and oranges. There must be something more substantial that I could be honored to do."

"The prayers and well wishes which accompany each flower and each orange are more important than anything else you could do. Please continue to keep us in your thoughts and prayers."

On her stationery were written the names of the members in her shopping expedition. Each was underlined in a bold hand and followed by a list from which she never wavers. She does not come to window shop or buy on a whim. She comes to purchase stock and take it home.

"First for Josette, white bra, 36B, Vanity Fair, Number 9172."

I carry all the "Yankee" brands; they are to Saint what French underwear must be to the Midwest. I got her the bra. She examined it and gestured to Josette to examine it. They nodded.

"Three pair, hip-huggers, mixed colors, your line, size six."

She examined them. Josette examined them. They nodded.

"One long nightgown, yellow with white lace, size medium, please recommend."

She did not mean, show me five gowns to choose from. She meant for me to pick one for her within the stated parameters. I did so.

I saw the monster I had created from the corner of my eye. Usually steady paced, Maria-Elena was rushing through her customer in a frenzy. She sent me one of her "I am sorry I am not there to help you in your moment of need" looks. I vowed to smash her well-intentioned face in if she interrupted me on this sacred transaction. She knew better.

She shut the register with too much determination.

I handed Señora Cortez four pair, full brief, white, for Ramona to examine and excused myself politely. I moved a few paces to the left to head off the charging Maria-Elena. I was still within hearing distance of Señora Cortez and entourage. In an undertone, I told Maria-Elena that I needed the totals tallied since Monday on the monthly report.

She told me that she was sorry, but that she had done them already.

"Then the schedule for next month," I told her, although this month had only just started. "It must be done immediately."

"I am sorry, Rubia." She was wringing her hands. "I did it while you were away."

"Then the stock count on the year, Maria-Elena. It must be started at once."

"Again, I am sorry, Rubia, but it is already up to date."

Señora Cortez began to fidget.

I remained calm. "Then go count your fingers, Maria-Elena. But do something, anything, and leave me alone to handle this. Please."

She stepped right by me, apologizing, of course, and said to Señora Cortez, "Excuse me, please, but you can imagine the strain the Rubia has been under."

She continued wringing her hands. She cannot help herself. She *has* to help.

"...with her mother-in-law...with the events, the things happening at her house, Señora Cortez. We are concerned that she does not strain herself. May I continue to help you?"

"A more precise word, Señorita, is cancer," Señora Cortez said, placing one hand on her left breast prosthesis. "Cancer, not events or things. And I have not forgotten that Rubia's mother-in-law, a generous and lovely lady, is dying from it. Your concern is taken into account. But perhaps it is better that the Rubia has something to take her mind off her situation. Please allow her to continue."

Maria-Elena's mouth opened. I could not believe it. She was ready to answer the grand old lady back. I stuck my eyeballs halfway down her throat. I silently vowed to demote her to the back room to make lace with my three spidery fates except that they each make a much higher salary than Maria-Elena. She closed her mouth, but did not move away. She looked like a statue about to cry. I was obliged to walk around her each time I went to get the stock for Señora Cortez. I changed my silent vow and decided to promote her to manager at once whether she refused again or not. She once accused me of threatening her with promotion. So be it. I would carry out her imagined threat and promote her.

I could hardly wait until lunch time for a change in atmosphere. Maria-Elena did nothing but excuse herself and apologize for the rest of the morning. That is a horrible way to live. I know because I do it myself much of the time.

Santa del Rio has not fallen prey to the nine-to-five workday as the larger cities closer to civilization have. It continues, as it has for centuries, to function on its own time. Stores and municipal services in the city open anywhere from 9:00 to 10:00 A.M. They close again, except for restaurants, along the line of 1:00 to 4:00 P.M. for the large meal of the day and the siesta and reopen again until 7:00 or 8:00 P.M. I have never quite gotten used to the lack of fidelity to clocks here. I set my elegantly unreadable watch every day and never bother to look at it. Averaging little more than four and a half hours of sleep each night, I benefit greatly from lack of punctuality and the daily practice of siesta.

The three Spinning Marias usually wander off first near lunch time and are usually the last to return. I do not know where they wander off. I do not know where they live. Two of my salespersons pick up their children first at school before returning home to the rest of their families. They always arrive back here exhausted. Another, a widow, has a rigorous schedule of visting each of her eight children's homes on a rotating basis.

Maria-Elena goes to her small apartment, a fifteen-minute drive away. She is very proud of having her own apartment. And although I have never visited it—we are separated by twenty years and rarely socialize outside of work—I know that she has a right to be proud of it. It is most unusual for a young single female in a Spanish household to have her own place. Her parents treat it as a whim after she fought tooth and nail to get it, and keep her room reserved at home which is not far away and where Maria-Elena still spends most of her time.

Another Maria helps out in her family's small dinette a block away. I often grab a take-out lunch from there. It is too far away for me to go back home, unless I decide to leave for the day. After eating, I sleep in my office until the hustle and bustle builds up again from the returning Marias. It is a most pleasant way to center the day.

I was still very tired from the tranquilizer and from too much drugged sleep. Maria-Elena was still underfoot in an annoying puppy dog fashion.

"You shouldn't have come in today on your day off. Look how tired you are."

I didn't answer hoping she'd leave.

"Are you sure I can't help you, Rubia?"

"How can you help me sleep."

"Oh, but there must be something I can do."

"If you wish to accompany me for some lunch, you are most welcome. Perhaps we can discuss your promotion then."

"No. You must not go out. You must stay here and rest. If you are hungry, I'll go and bring some food back for you."

"No, I am not hungry."

"Well, here let me help you with that."

Shit, she was even helping me undress.

I stripped down to my slip. She smoothed my dress over the back of the chair. She put the sheet I keep on the shelf over the green couch and patted it for me. God save me. Was

she going to sing me a lullaby too? She started to hum a tune.
I lay down so she'd leave. She was still humming. I closed my
eyes. She finally left. I heard her lock the door.

Except that I was not tired anymore. I got up to take my
noon tranquilizer, but I didn't take it. They didn't have to run
my life when they weren't around. I lay down again. I closed
my eyes only to have a vague sense of fear compete for my
time. Maybe I was still confused from the morning tranquilizer. The edges seemed blurry. But the tune she was humming,
there was something about it. Or maybe it was my "chronic
insomnia" and I knew from years of trying to fight it late at
night that sleep just doesn't come to those who wait silently
in the darkness and demand it like the obedience of a naughty
child. I slipped my dress back on and left by the back door.
Federico had the jeep, so I didn't know where I was going.

Perhaps the details were not evident to me until later. But
Federico was too insistent that I not go to work on my usual
day off. Maria-Elena was too surprised to see me on my usual
day off. She was too insistent that I take it easy and rest at
siesta time and not wander about town. She practically took
my clothes off and patted the couch for me and hummed that
damn tune, "To Love Somebody"—that was what she was
humming.

After I left the shop, I wandered around town for a long
time, hazily following the notes to that tune.

I saw the jeep parked in the residential section.

I saw Federico come out of the small apartment house
that I think Maria-Elena lives in. I didn't let him see me. I
took a taxi back to the store. When Maria-Elena came back
after lunch she was too freshly showered. But it didn't matter.
The lingering perfume she wore was of sex and a smell of sex
too familiar to me.

I followed her, sniffing.

"What are you doing?" she said.

"Smelling," I answered.

"You are perhaps more upset than we thought after having seen your ghost and being on tranquilizers."

"And how do you know I saw a ghost? And how do you know I was on tranquilizers!"

"You told me, didn't you?" and her voice trailed off. "Yes, you told me yesterday," she said too firmly.

"I wasn't on tranquilizers yesterday."

I had to wait over an hour sitting in the park for school to let out. I could have taken a taxi, but the only thing I could think of when I ran out of the shop was to go to my children. I rode back with them on the school bus. I had never done this before. I tried to act like it was normal for a grown woman to sit between her two children on the miniature seats and cry.

10

≈ ≈ ≈ ≈ ≈ ≈ ≈ ≈ ≈ ≈ ≈

"Dear Santa del Rio."
"Dear Ann Landers."
"Hail Mary, full of grace," I cry aloud after I have closed the door to my room. Our room.

I cry with fury.

I plot the murder.

But whose? Maria-Elena's or Federico's. Maybe I'll kill them both in bed together.

I weep with rage.

Crimes of passion are treated lightly in Latin countries. But perhaps not lightly enough if committed by an Anglo. They don't think we are capable of real passion let alone crimes of passion. My hair will look too blond in the black dress on the witness stand. I'll dye it black after the murder. I'll get brown contact lenses.

I cry aloud.

Dear Ann Landers.

Blessed are thou among women.

I think. But will Ann Landers answer a letter to South America from a person who has not read her column since she was a teenager. And will Mary answer a prayer from a person who only goes to church on special occasions with a new outfit.

Hail Ann Landers full of grace.

Dear Hail Mary.

11

They are so perfect. I wonder how there ever could have been a time when I wanted to shove their crying little bodies into someone else's arms while I wondered "Why me, God?" and meant it in any language. How I could have lifted my arms to heaven in exasperation with too many diapers, sniffles and teething mouths. How I could have gagged so hard when changing their diapers and then felt so guilty about gagging, acting on some misinformed old wives' tale that your own kid's shit should smell sweeter to you than any other shit. How I could have yelled such obscenities at the quiet white nuns while they prayerfully urged these creatures from my body!

They are so perfect. Their little hands moved so lovingly to catch a tear drop, to move a strand of hair from my face. Their little mouths moved so gently to offer casual explanations which quieted the bus driver and moved the other little girls away. Their little cousins were scared. From the moment they saw me rushing through the little gate where the convent school doors open out, the Niña, the Pinta and the Santa Maria started sniveling and asking half-formed questions.

"Be quiet now. Leave her alone and go sit on the other side of the bus," Margherita told them. I wondered if they also would be so brave if it was their own mother on the bus.

I was not sniffling; I was in a full weep even if I was doing it as softly as I could remember to. Patricia replaced the kleenex in my hand with one from the little girl across the aisle.

Margherita asked only one question, "Is it grandmother?"

"No," I told her, "it is not grandmother."

They took deep sighs into their little bodies and coura-
geously fought off the inclination to join in my mysterious
hysteria. They sat, one on each side of me, and acted as if it
was an everyday thing that I should join them on the little
yellow bus and cry. And there was no way to tell them—they
were wearing blue seersucker jumpers with the Sacred Virgin
of the Rosary tattooed to the pockets. Even after a hard day's
play down in the stables, they have never smelled less fresh
than a leaf crumpled in one's hand. There was no way to tell
them that I followed Maria-Elena around for an hour after lunch
and caught a too-familiar smell of sex reeking discreetly from
her person.

"Thank you," I told the old bus driver when we got off.

"Thank you," Margherita said.

"Thank you," Patricia said.

"Should we come also?" Rosa's eldest called out.

"Of course. This is your home, silly. Where else would
you go?" Margherita said.

I was through the front door and halfway up the stairs
when I heard them still hushing their cousins and casually
offering explanations on how I didn't feel too good at work and
came home early with them to a surprised Rosa and a reverent
Ada, who probably thought the whole thing was just another
manifestation of my newly annointed communication with the
not-yet-dead saints.

"It's probably her hormones," Margherita said. Margherita! who has at least a year, probably two, to go before a
hormone even enters her little body. They are so perfect. Both
of them.

I went to my room. Our room. I cried uncontrollably and
pounded the pillows. I tired of crying and pounding. Perhaps

by divine intervention through Ann Landers or the Virgin Mary, I decided to go to see the Señora.

A visiting nurse, the same one who tried to sedate me two nights ago, was knitting in the arm chair.

"Get out," I told her.

"But Señora, it is impossible. You are not on the list."

"Go check the refrigerators and the desks, I'm on the list now."

"What?"

"Get out!"

In a flurry of white uniform and pink wool, she grabbed her knitting bag and left. "I'll report this to Señora Rosa," she added before I shut the door. I locked it behind her.

Half the room looked like a hospital, half like a florist and fruit store and smelt like a...yes, like a funeral parlor. There were orchids and oranges, medicine bottles and tubes, all neatly organized and arranged. The Señora looked like a tiny doll propped up on the massive lace bed. She did not look dead, she looked inanimate. In my own house, or rather in the many different apartment houses in which we grew up, nothing was so organized, nothing placed so precisely so. When the clutter would get too messy, my mother would decide it was time to move to a different apartment. My father changed jobs like my mother moved our apartments. The only constant was the piano upon which my mother still gives lessons. I never got past "The Spinning Song." But my older sister is a concert pianist with the Philharmonic and yet, according to my mother, who prefers show tunes over classical music, her only prize pupil is a keyboard player in a rock band that never made it to the top forty. If it was my mother who was dying, it would be different, I know. I can picture how it would happen. She would be sitting at the piano playing something from South Pacific. She would do something sudden, like play a variation on a chord or burp, and then slump over the piano, dead.

"Daddy," I would say when he would come up the steps and open the door, "Mom is slumped over the piano. I think she is dead."

"I don't think so, Susie Honey," he would tell me. "I think she is probably just tired." Then he would kiss the back of her neck and pat her ass like he always did when he came home and walk by her into the kitchen.

"Abuela, are you sleeping?"

Her eyes were closed. She was propped up almost into a sitting position on the big bed. Her dark hair was piled in a neat bun on top of her head. Her skin was pale.

I moved the tables and stands away and pulled up one of the small chairs not far from the bed. She opened her eyes and smiled softly with no surprise that it was me or that I was crying.

"I want to sleep, too," I told her. "Or at least I don't know what I want to do." She closed her eyes again and seemed to drift away.

"Yes, it's true, I want to sleep because I don't know what else to do."

My own words seemed to have comforted me. I was surprised that I could still speak when I wasn't crying. I wrung the kleenex in my hand. She didn't seem to be listening. She didn't seem like she was still connected to this world. It didn't seem that anything I could say would have connected to her.

"My husband, your son, is having an affair. It is not what you are thinking. This is not one night of passion or a quickie over cocktails. He might have had a few of those for all I know, or at least he could have with that tourist from Canada four years ago. I am talking about an affair, a mistress. And with whom? No, perhaps you already know with whom. Perhaps everyone knows except me. Oh God, I took her right after she graduated from that damn convent school. I taught her the books, the right way to wear her hair, what clothes were professional. I always bring her back a little present from New York when I visit there. She wears underwear from the store. *My* store. I brought her back a little pink lace pillow from Saks Fifth last year. I bet it's on the bed where they..."

I cried for a little while. I moved the chair closer. The Señora's eyes were still closed. She had not moved.

"Oh, I know. I know that this is all very silly of me. That this is no cause for dramatics. That it is only natural in the course of things that a husband should have an affair after fifteen years of marriage. It's traditional. But I have always loved him and trusted him even after the newness wore off and I never even suspected her. That other time, the time I'm not positive about, with the Canadian, was only because he was with his brother-in-law and they were drunk from the festival."

This is easy, I thought. The words sounded so lucid, like a letter to Ann Landers.

"Oh, this must not seem like such a big deal to you with what you're going through, and I know I should not burden you with this, but you and I have always talked. Not about things like this maybe but...affairs are just so commonplace. It all seems so typically male and accepted, so typically macho. It is almost like there is nothing to be angry about or at least not surprised about. It is so accepted. And that makes me feel even more angry.

"Maybe I am just crazy lately. That's what everyone around here is saying anyway. A few months ago I was driving through the center of town to get to the hospital to see you. I was doing the speed limit or even a little slower because the traffic was moving slowly, and out from behind one of the parked cars jumped a young man. He couldn't have been more than sixteen. I slammed on the brakes and missed hitting him by less than a foot. He was clearly at fault but that didn't stop me from feeling terrible, of course. If I had been going five miles

an hour faster.... And such a close call took my breath away.
His face was close and so young. A line of cars behind me had
also to slam on their brakes and I heard tires screeching and
the man just stood there. I thought that he also was in shock
until he very deliberately kissed the tips of his fingers and
placed them on his ass with a little wiggle and a sarcastic smile.
I meant to kill him for his arrogance. I even took my foot off
the brake and would have slammed it on the gas except that
the car behind me let out an annoyed honk and brought me
back to my senses.

"I am so angry. I just feel like packing my bags and leaving
Federico and going home. I feel like I don't have a home
anymore. I feel like..."

She opened her eyes. She seemed to be trying to say
something with her eyes. Her eyes looked at her hand. Her
hand motioned for me to move closer. I was practically on the
bed to hear her faint voice whisper distinctly, "Cut off his
balls."

"Pardon me," I said. I already knew what she had said.
Her whisper was most distinct. It's just that I had never heard
her say anything like that before. I didn't even know she knew
such words. I didn't even think she was listening.

She closed her eyes. She seemed to return to the world
of the inanimate.

I sat back and thought about cutting off balls—Federico's
balls, the young man on the street's balls, anybody's balls. But
each time I thought about cutting off balls, I couldn't help
picturing what was connected to those balls, like Federico's
fat cock making its way into that dark triangle between plump
thighs that Maria-Elena must have, that I had never pictured
before, and the image made me start to cry again.

"This is impossible, Abuela. How could you say such a
thing?"

Her eyes opened again and she motioned with her hand

to come closer. I moved my head a little closer.

Her words came in breathy spurts, "How do you think...my husband has...water...limp."

Oh dear God, I thought, the secret of my father-in-law's limp!

"You cut off your husband's balls under water?"

"No, I am...I need water."

When I held the glass up to her mouth, she hardly sipped it, only tasted it. Once. Twice. She had barely taken enough to warrant a swallow.

"More, Abuela?"

My mind raced with visions of her fragile white hand, now with a tube in it, bearing a stiletto against my father-in-law's balls. Perhaps there was a rose in her mouth.

"No more."

I replaced the glass next to the crystal pitcher.

She motioned for me to come closer again. I did so.

"Closer."

My head was almost touching hers. I was kneeling on the bed.

"You must stay here," she said and drifted far away.

I tried to concentrate on what she said about staying here to take my mind off my father-in-law's balls. I was not sure if she meant that I should stay in this house and not go away, or if I was to stay with her in the room, or if she meant that I should just stay where I was on the bed, which seemed absurd but not all that absurd because I was very tired from so much crying and so many shocks. I decided to stay where I was and lie down until I was sure she was asleep. My head was on the other end of the long pillow. Each time I thought of Federico I thought of his father's limp. One or both balls? He only limps on the left. It was unbelievable that the Señora would do a thing like that. It was even more unbelievable than the odor I detected from Maria-Elena. I fell asleep.

12

I have been a prisoner for two days now. The only reason that I have not been sedated is because they think I was sedated when I fell asleep in the Señora's bed. I did not tell them that I hadn't taken any of the assigned tranquilizers since that morning. They wouldn't have believed me anyway if I had told them that the Señora had told me to stay in her bed, or at least I thought that was what she meant.

I am confined to my side of the house. My meals are brought to me here. Ada places them reverently on the desk in the upstairs sitting room. I give her information on my holy vision of last week and she gives me current information of the daily proceedings of the household. I am allowed down to the kitchen after dinner under heavy security to mix the medicine. Margherita and Patricia sleep two doors down the hall as usual. They play Scrabble with me at night. Federico is sleeping downstairs in the den or so Ada tells me.

I have heard since how they found me sleeping in the Señora's bed. The visiting nurse with the mass of pink wool had not reported me directly to Rosa, but to her nursing supervisor when she got back to the office in town. The supervisor naturally thought that the "crazy Señora" who had driven away her knitting nurse had been Rosa, and being used to dealing with Rosa, she did not think twice.

Dinner preparations had been delayed as Rosa took the phone call from the supervisor.

"Of course," Rosa had said. "You can send over the next nurse on duty. Why not?"

"No," Rosa said, she had not been unhappy with the performance of the nurse who knits and sent her home early.

The supervisor didn't belabor the point. But Rosa smelt something amiss and went to check on her mother with Ada hot on her heels. Finding the door locked, Rosa had knocked softly thinking maybe the nurse had fallen asleep but not wishing to disturb her mother. She knocked a little louder and called out but still no answer. She sent Ada to find one of the old master keys which took some time since there were many desks to search through. Federico had returned in the interim and asked Ada where I was. It only took a second when Rosa shook me awake for me to realize the severity of the situation.

"Where is the nurse who was on duty?" Rosa whispered harshly.

"She was angry that I was on the sitting schedule, too," I lied.

Rosa clucked her tongue.

"She said that if you did not have enough confidence in her ability to take care of the patient by herself then she would leave. I tried to tell her that it wasn't that, but only that it was important to have family around also."

"But you weren't on the schedule."

"But yes, Rosa, I was."

"If you please, that was the old schedule, not the one I've made since you saw your vision."

I had moved over to the chair by then.

"But Rosa, that was the only schedule I knew of. I am sorry. I didn't know you had changed it." I continued lying; I didn't even know I was on the old schedule.

"I had to change it because the doctor had put you on the tranquilizers. But that is not important now. What were you doing sleeping on the bed with my mother? And why did you lock the door, Rubia?"

"I didn't. The nurse must have locked the door behind her and she was angry and calling you a crazy woman. I felt so dizzy after the argument and from the tranquilizers that I must have fallen on the bed. The medicine is too strong for me. You were right to take me off the schedule. But I didn't know I was off and I felt it was my duty and I figured it would be OK, since I thought the nurse would be here too."

"You should have called for help," Rosa said.

"I could not. I was very weak. I tried to get up several times, but my legs were too weak. You must have an emergency phone put in here. And you must speak to the nursing service. You are the only one who can handle them."

"Yes, of course, maybe you are right." She started sweating and mumbling about a phone and a batch of new and better nurses. Her head was popping with ideas for confronting the nursing supervisor and the idea of getting an emergency phone looked like it definitely appealed to her. The phone company is notoriously bad here. The lines are down more than they are working at the edge of the jungle.

"Yes," Rosa said, looking at her sleeping mother, "maybe a new phone for emergencies..."

When someone is dying and there is nothing you can do to really help, the thought of doing anything, no matter how remote, which connects you to that person, takes on new dimensions.

"Yes, maybe a nice white phone over by her bed," she continued as I sneaked out of the room.

It was only when I saw Ada standing so humbly on the landing and Federico standing so innocently next to her that I blew my exit.

"Whore! Traitor! Scumbag! Pig!" I remember yelling in any language that came to mind.

"You piece of shit!" I remember. I do not remember that

they had to pull me off his neck and that there were marks left on his throat; Ada told me that later. I don't remember how I got back to my room either. I do know that Federico came into my room, our room, and I remember hissing how Maria-Elena stunk of him and he told me that I was crazy. And I told him everything else and he denied that, too. And how I wanted to believe him more than anything else. But the closer he came to me, the more I could smell him and his smell only confirmed my memory and then I remembered the tune she was humming. He denied ever having heard that tune either. But when I tried to call Maria-Elena on the telephone, he put his finger down on the button and said, "Can't you try to be discreet. My mother is dying."

Then I threw the telephone and the chair and the books and he left, and I threw more books and the vase the Señora gave us on our tenth wedding anniversary and the table and I remember Rosa screaming in the hall, "Oh, when will the effects of these tranquilizers wear off!"

I fell asleep in the rubble. I did not know I was capable of such violence. I was so ashamed. I should have been more sensible and just cut off his balls.

Everything hurt when I woke up. The floor where Ada gently walked as she quietly picked through the rubble shook the bed and hurt my head. The pillow hurt my head. The heat was so heavy that it hurt my head. My head filled the entire room. The entire universe.

"Rubia, are you better now?" Rosa whispered, which hurt my head. Then Rosa pulled back the curtains and the grey light pounded my head.

"Drugs," I screamed. "I need drugs!"

"*Dios mio*, we have addicted her," Rosa said to Ada.

"Drugs!" I said.

Doctor Garcia hurt my head by making me answer questions and then rotated my head back and forth which sent tears to my eyes.

"Drugs," I told him. "I need drugs."

"No, you just have a migraine. It will go away. Just rest. I cannot give you any medicine because they tell me you reacted very badly to the tranquilizers and they could have even precipitated your headache."

He mercifully closed the curtains when he left.

When I woke up, the pain in my head was less but my heart hurt. I told Federico to go away when he knocked on the door and he did.

Later, Señor Rodriguez knocked on the door and asked me how I was feeling.

"Better," I told him.

"Good. If you feel up to it, you can come down and mix the medicine."

"I can't. I am a prisoner."

"What are you talking about? The door is open. It has been open all the time."

So with my father-in-law guarding me, I was led down to the empty kitchen. He sat and watched me. I pulled out the vials and jars and the droppers. I couldn't help looking at his crotch.

"How is Abuela today?" I asked him, as he caught me staring between his legs.

"What?"

"How is the Señora? I have to know so I can give her the right formula."

"Oh, she is the same, like yesterday. Just sleeping all of the time as is expected."

"Thank you. Oh, by the way, how did you hurt your leg?"

He pulled out a long cigar and lit it. The smoke rose past his long eyes and great shock of white hair.

"In the war."

"In what war?"

"In the wars for our country."

"Whom did you fight against?"

"I fought against the Greens, we called them, because they printed their propanganda on green paper."

"And what was your side called?"

"I don't remember if we had a name."

"What did you stand for?"

"For our country."

"What did the other side stand for?"

"For the country."

"Which country?"

"The same country."

"What was the difference then?"

"We won."

"Yes, but what would have happened to your country if the other side had won?"

"No one will ever know. I think that I would have been killed though, or put in prison for fighting on the wrong side."

"That is not what I mean, Abuelo. What did you fight for? What was the difference in your philosophy?"

"We did not fight for philosophy. We fought because we needed a new leader and because we are men."

"I am sure I don't understand. But just tell me how you got your limp."

"In the war."

I added an extra splash of Ada's second cousin's cure for the war in which Señor Rodriguez said he got his limp.

"I will walk you back to your room, if you are finished now," he said.

13

≈ ≈ ≈ ≈ ≈ ≈ ≈ ≈ ≈ ≈ ≈

I have been a prisoner for three days now. The pain in my head is gone, but my heart hurts all the time.

I want the pain to go away. I don't want to be part of this. I want my name back. Federico knocked on the door last night.

"Rubia, I want to talk to you."

"That is not my name," I said. "Go away."

And he did.

It is not so bad being a prisoner. You can't get out, but some things can't come in either. But why does he go away so quickly when I tell him to?

I have principles. I am no longer Rubia. I just want to be Susan Thompson like my mother named me. How disappointed I had been when I learned "Rubia" had nothing to do with a precious jewel but meant "Blondie." We had been married for a few months. I had never met his family.

"So this is the Rubia," Rosa said as we met in the airport. I had on my good blue jeans and *South America on Five Dollars a Day* tucked under my arm. I thought we were going to live on a farm with Indians, not on a hacienda with Indian slave labor and Rosa.

Rosa touched my hair.

"Is it real?" she asked.

It is not bad, they told me. "Blondie" is not a cheap name in Spanish. It is a nice name. I let myself be deceived from

84

the very start. I even named my store "Rubia's" years later. I can see each label, special ordered and exported to the finest of designer shops across the world, each curving script—"Rubia's."

No not Rubia. Not even Suzanna. Only Susan. I will have to get a divorce. This balls business is absurd. The Señora must really be delirious. She couldn't have cut even one ball off even if my father-in-law's war story does sound suspicious. And what would I accomplish if I did cut off Federico's balls? Add another limping man to South America to tell tall tales about wars? The divorce will be hard on the girls. They have come with me to New York a few times to visit my family, but this is their home and their heritage. The hacienda is all they have ever really known. And Federico has been a good father to them. If he was as disappointed as the rest of the family that they were not boys, he never showed it for an instant. But we will have to go, the girls and I, far away, back to New York. I have thought it over. I can sell the business. I have had offers before. I can even keep an interest if I want. I will have to wait until the Señora dies, of course. That much is only her due out of respect. Although there have been times when I did not show her respect, I have always loved her. And now, I have become just like the others waiting for her to die.

There is a feeling peculiar to a woman's first childbirth that comes after the first transition of labor. It is seen in the eyes first when nothing looks familiar anymore, after the relief and excitement of finally being in real labor is over, after the long rest periods between contractions become alarmingly shorter. There seems no time to rest between movement. No time to breathe. No time to acclimate yourself to changing situations. There comes the fear bordering on panic that whispers in the ear over and over again—there is no way out of this. There is no turning back now. You are going to do this whether you like it or not and you will then be responsible, only you, forever and ever.

It was like that when I got off the plane that first day in South America. It is like that now.

14

I have been a prisoner for four days. It must be near
dawn. It is very dark. The light from over the patio
door illuminates a tiny corner of the courtyard below
my window. The hot humid air does not fill the empty spaces.
The white ceiling fan moves the air, but does not fill the empty
spaces. I keep the old yellow dog here with me now. When it
gets too lonely, I call him. He gets up to let me pat him, wags
his tail arthritically, turns slowly in a circle, and lies down like
a bag of cement on the wooden floor.

I told Federico tonight. I was very calm. He denied
everything again and said only that he will not even discuss
such a matter while his mother is dying. It was like a long
monologue without argument. I told him that I hadn't realized
our relationship had deteriorated. That I might have been more
forgiving if it hadn't been Maria-Elena. That this was not only
painful, but an insult to me to think he had involved someone
from my business also. That I felt I deserved better. How
could it come to this, I said. I cried a little then. We have
been through so much together. We had crossed over the
bounds of culture and language to love each other.

I told him that I saw no other way but a divorce and that
I would wait until his mother was "over being sick." The girls
will come with me, of course. We will go to New York, I told
him. I will sell the business and the girls could come back to
visit him. I wanted nothing more from him in terms of a

settlement.

"How can you sit here like a rock with your head in your hands when I say all this or am I just a fool not to have realized sooner?"

He looked up and ran his hand through his dark curls.

"Because I told you. None of this is true. Except to deny it. I will not even think about this while my mother is dying. It will be different 'after,' Rubia, and you will know that none of this is true."

I was crying a little then, too. He got up.

"Do you still want me to sleep downstairs in the den again?"

"Yes, Federico. It would be easier that way."

I alternate by the second between love and hate. Either way, everything about Federico has become important. Every shadow, every gesture, every memory either damns or redeems him.

It was late afternoon on a Sunday. We met in a bar down the street from the U.N. during an anti-war demonstration. Federico was at the demonstration to see what his Yankee college roommates did on a Sunday afternoon. He was at the bar because it was the only thing along the peace march that smelled of home.

I was at the demonstration because I was sincerely against the Vietnam War and because I am a faddist. I was at the bar because I was supposed to meet my girlfriends there after the rally. I was an hour early because I was wearing surplus army boots, which were the latest, and they hurt my feet. The bar was called "Five Flags" or something close to that and each table was decorated with tiny U.N. souvenir flags. I sat at a booth with the menu in my hands savoring the soft padded seat and the late autumn sunshine pouring through the window. The crisp smell of autumn came threw the open door.

"What's your pleasure?" the waiter said.

"A glass of white wine for now. I'm waiting for some friends," I was careful to add.

"This is compliments of the gentleman at the bar," he said when he returned with the wine.

I blushed furiously and stumbled over a thank you, not knowing what else to do. I took a sip nonchalantly, wondering what kind of pervert would send a drink to a woman wearing army boots. I was sorry that I had not been paying more attention to the bar and less to the sunlight and smell of fall. I crossed off the tall dark man at the far side of the bar with a picket sign by his side because he looked my age and therefore not old enough to do something which I considered out of a 1940's black and white movie. The three men standing over the woman in a pink dress and blond wig were certainly not suave enough. That left the bartender and waiter, neither of whom looked like they could have cared if the sky fell in, and the back of a man in a blue suit with salt and pepper hair. I scrutinized the blue suit carefully from the tips of his black patent leather shoes to the tilt of the back of his head, trying to catch an angle of his face. A man in patent leather shoes might be attracted to army boots. He must have felt someone staring at him and he turned with a start and gave me a sly smile and a broad wink. The gray in his hair was not premature. He was old enough to be my grandfather. He was probably a WWI veteran. I bent down under the table to pick up an imaginary anything. From the underside of the world I saw a protest sign being propped next to mine.

"May I help for you to find something?" said a thick Latin accent.

"No, I am just tired and waiting for some friends," I replied, having already thought of an answer if anyone asked me what I was doing by myself in the bar.

"Ah, so you have fallen over then?"

"No, of course not," I said and sat back up.

"Yes, this picking is hard work and makes for tired and your feet are heavy, no? May I sit down, too, if you please, since we are both picking?"

"Look, mister, I'm not a pick-up," I said to the Latin man now hesitantly standing at my side.

"I am sorry. My English is not too much. My name is Federico Rodriguez-Garcia. How are you?"

From across the room, the face of the man in the blue suit seemed to have frozen in a wink.

"Did you buy me this drink?" I said to Federico Rodriguez-Garcia.

"No..."

"Well, sit down then," I said, staring across at the blue suit. He turned back around to the bar as Federico sat down in the booth with me.

"Thank God," I said.

"Do you want a drink then?" He looked at my full glass of wine.

"No, thank you."

"Ah, you are thanking God because you found what you were looking for under the table."

"Yes, and I didn't even lose anything." I smiled. He was incredibly handsome in a dark kind of way. "Oh, that's what you meant about the hard work of 'picking up.'"

"I'm sorry my English is not so good. Let me repeat, the picking in the street for no war is hard work for a lady, no?" He pointed to his sign propped against the chair by mine— "NO GO" in red block letters over a black peace sign.

"Oh. Oh yes. The picketing. The picket signs from the demonstration."

"One is present then and the other past tense?"

It turned out that we attended the same college, different

campus.

We were married in the spring, two weeks after gradu-
ation. We spent most of the summer in a small rented room
in Cape Cod living frugally on his allowance and the money
my parents had given us on our wedding. When the town
began to clear out at the end of August, Federico said let's
go to my home.

Why not, I thought. I had never met his family. Why not
embark on a new adventure to South America. I must have
been high on suntan lotion or love. Yes, we were voraciously
in love and splendidly horny. Water surrounded us and we
glistened in the sun. He was so dark and handsome against
the white sheets and the white sand and the white sails. Yes,
even once in a rented sailboat. His cock was like a polished
baton of dark wood.

It will not be so difficult I know now thinking of that
afternoon in the sailboat and that gleaming baton. Even under
heavy guard I can slip one of the kitchen knives into a pocket,
and I control the medicine. Enough morphine in some food or
drink will keep him content until it has been done.

15

≈ ≈ ≈ ≈ ≈ ≈ ≈ ≈ ≈ ≈ ≈

I am still imprisoned. I am not sure what day of my imprisonment this is but I've been too busy thinking about other things. When I think of what I am about to do, my hands tremble and my teeth chatter. So I do not think of it often, only of my plan which keeps me calm and keeps the pain in my heart away. I took one of the small sharp blades Ada uses for paring. The evening before last I decided to put the plan into action. I was called to mix the medicine not long after dinner. I was under not only the watchful eyes of Señor Rodriguez in the kitchen but also Rosa, Ada, and Ada's second cousin's niece, who is here as a housemaid replacing Ada's first cousin's daughter, who is home taking care of her sister's four small children whose mother ran away to join a convent or "so she said," or so the conversation went and attention being diverted as I ground some extra morphine tablets and slipped them into an envelope in my pocket.

Accomplished. And cocksure enough to focus the attention on myself, I said to Rosa, "You see, you could run away and join the convent, too. You don't even have to be single or a virgin."

"No. No. No," they all said missing what I had intended as sarcasm. And then they explained how no one really believed that Ada's first cousin's daughter's sister had really run away to join the convent but had only said that ("Such a sacrilege to say," Rosa added) as she had been seen in town with a young

man from out of town, which was a shame since she had four
lovely children and her husband was always so nice to her
except when he was drunk....

Somewhere along there, smugly patting my morphine
pocket, I went cold with fear.

Back in my room, I paced furiously while trying to wring
the cold from my hands.

"What am I doing!" I said to myself. "Cutting off balls is
one thing..."

"Remember," I said back to myself, "you've been over
this already. You don't have to cut them off. Just a little nick
to remind him. Just a *little* limp so he will be too embarrassed
to call the police."

"OK. That's one thing," I replied. "But putting an unknown
quantity of a drug whose effects you are not even sure of into
his body is a whole other thing."

I went over the scenario in my head again. First, I bring
him some coffee. I will definitely be permitted to bring him
coffee even though I am under surveillance, because it is a
woman's place to bring her husband coffee (except that this
coffee will be laced with morphine which would be frowned
upon even in more liberated societies).

"Here, dear, here is some coffee," I will say. "Perhaps I
have been too harsh lately."

He will drink it and say that it tastes funny.

I will tell him that I'm sorry but there's a new housemaid
helping Ada: a new twist, I was going to tell him that I was
sorry but that I made it all by myself and he knows I don't
cook well. I will make small talk while I watch him drink the
coffee. Then I will leave. Then I will wait until everyone is
asleep. I will tiptoe down to the kitchen first to make sure the
coast is clear. Then to the den to give him a very slight limp.
First, I will turn on the small desk lamp. Then I will talk to
him and nudge him on the couch to make sure that he is deeply

asleep. But in this new scenario he's more than deeply asleep. He's cold and dead. Too much morphine. I definitely need a new plan.

So I calculated that if the Señora weighs about the same as I do, then I should take about the same amount and see what the effects are on me. I also calculated that it was possible that the Señora had built up some kind of resistance to the drug so a little less than her dose or maybe a little more than that to be sure. I drank the dose in my after dinner coffee. I slept soundly through the night and the next day.

They tried twice, I think, to wake me yesterday and I told them to go away that I had a headache. I was paralyzed. I was awake and aware some of the time, but I was unable to move. Exactly the effect I was looking for. I scheduled Frederico for twice that dosage plus a pinch for good luck for the next night.

I bathed in perfume that evening. I loosely piled my hair on my head and pulled down a few strands to grace the back of my neck. With the morphine envelope in the top of my slip, I put on a soft voile dress the color of pale blue to match my eyes. I checked on the girls who were just going to bed.

"Are you going out tonight, Mama?" they asked.

As I was coming out of the girls' room, I met Ada in the hall coming out of the sitting room with my barely touched dinner tray.

"You look beautiful," she said. "Like a new woman."

"You look different, Rubia," Señor Rodriquez said as he cut me off at the bottom of the stairs. "You must have needed that sleep."

I nodded, too stunned to speak. Did it show? Did I look different as a ball-cutter than as a regular person?

"Please be gentle with Rosa tonight," my father-in-law continued. "Juan Ortega was angry with her this morning over God knows what this time and left and said he was never coming back. Federico and I found him this afternoon at one of the tourist bars, drunk. He said he'd come back when and if he felt like it. And I didn't beg him. He is not back yet. So, if you please, be kind."

"Yes, Abuelo," I said, feeling very kind.

The kitchen was quiet. The new housemaid finished the dishes and left. Ada said good night a little later. Rosa drank coffee and watched me make the medicine. I was using more cocaine and more of Ada's cousin's cure and less morphine to make up for the missing pills. But Rosa didn't notice. She was mostly listening to the sounds of the night outside. She would get up and wring her hands by the window. Señor Rodriquez sat in the high-backed wooden chair in the corner blowing tendrils of white smoke from his cigar. He watched Rosa with sad eyes. None of us said much.

"Is Federico in the den?" I asked as I was finishing up.

"Yes, he is in the den," the Señor said lifting his eyebrow.

"I will bring him some of that coffee, I think."

My voice trembled.

Rosa grabbed by hand. I almost fainted...

"It is only right. At least he is here..." My breath came back. "You look very nice. I wondered why," she said.

I made a little tray and put a piece of cake on it too.

I stopped at the hall table as if to fix my hair. There was no one around. I stirred the powdered morphine into the coffee.

"Federico, may I come in?"

"Yes, Rubia, come in."

"Here," I said thrusting the tray at him. He put it on the coffee table and sat back down on the couch. I sat stiffly in the arm chair accross from him. We did not speak for a moment.

Ada or Rosa must have certainly been pampering him. The portable TV was set up in the corner and droned softly, competing with the large portable fan. A potted plant from the courtyard had been moved to a corner of the room and the couch was already made up with freshly ironed sheets and fluffy pillows. The curtains were drawn back from the sliding glass door which opened to the courtyard, and the smell of roses and rotting vegetation, heavy on the air, flooded the room. Federico looked genuinely sad. My heart softened. Did I have a right to inflict even the tiniest limp on this man because delightful memories of a day on a sailboat some fifteen years ago had, by contrast, saddened my confused heart? Against the fresh white sheets on this couch, he still looked so dark and handsome. His dark chest was naked over his work pants. Small beads of sweat glistened and caught in the patch of hair in the center of his chest. He was holding in his stomach. He ran his hand through his curly hair as he always did when he was nervous.

"You have heard about Juan Ortega then," he said lifting his head towards the tray.

You bastard, I thought. My heart hardened. He thought that I was bringing him coffee as a conciliatory measure to prevent him from leaving as Rosa's husband had.

My voice no longer trembled. "Yes, I have heard about Juan Ortega. It was nice of you and your father to go to bring him back. But he has done this many times. He will be back before long as always."

"Who knows, Rubia, maybe this time he will be gone for good." He made his eyes larger and sadder. "He says that he is tired of it."

"Yes, Federico, maybe you are right. But please eat some cake," making my eyes look rounder and more humble.

"You are not joining me?"

"Oh, no. Thank you. I have already taken mine in the kitchen."

Like a good wife, I added in my head.

"The cake is very dry."

"Yes, Ada has a new assistant, as you know."

"Yes, and Ada should show her how to make a cup of coffee too. This is on the bitter side to say the least."

"Yes, but one needs something to wash down that dry cake and besides she is very easily insulted and when she gets insulted Ada gets insulted and Rosa and Ada start up again. You know how women are! Ha, Ha!"

"Yes, he said and gulped down the rest of his coffee.

Maybe he should limp in both legs, I thought.

I took the tray to leave.

"You are going so soon, *mi amor?*"

"Yes, Federico, but this was a good start, no?"

"Yes. Good night, Rubia."

Rosa was wringing her hands by the window. In her black dress, which made her look even hotter, she looked like she was wringing out her sweat.

"Is everything all right?"

"Yes, Rosa, for a start."

I rinsed the cup and saucer.

"Good night."

"Good night."

"Sleep well," Señor Rodriquez said through the smoke.

That was easy, I thought up in my room, easier than those imaginary letters to Ann Landers. Luckily, I had not thought of an outfit for the second phase of my plan so that occupied the next few hours. I finally dressed in jeans, sneakers, and a navy pullover and tucked my hair into a dark scarf on the back of my head. Practical. But in the mirror, I looked like a burglar. All wrong. If I was caught downstairs by the den, it would be better to look seductive and not like I was stealing silverware. So I tried on matching negligee after matching negligee—I have plenty of them—to kill time and to make it just perfect. The house had been quiet for a long time. Even if Rosa was worried about her husband, she probably couldn't stay up past ten o'clock if she wanted to. I had seen the inside light from the kitchen go out some time before.

Finally, I had decided. I put the hot rollers back into my hair and then brushed it all over to the side long and wavy. I had chosen lace, one of my own designs woven with the power of the Spinning Marias, the color of ripe burgundy. My skin felt soft and pink against the gown. My nipples peaked from behind the woven flowers. The robe tied with a silk ribbon. It was getting very late. I placed the knife in the elastic at the cuff of the robe. My love. My only love.

I was halfway down the dark stairs before I realized that I had no coordinated footwear on. In fact, I had no shoes on at all.

Was it right without shoes!

In a minute there was time to turn back and forget the whole thing. The cold blade pressed against my wrist where it rested beneath the cuff. This is not an elaborate sacrificial offering, I told myself. This was only going to be a little reminder and perhaps did not warrant high heels.

There is always an outside light on over the back door of the kitchen which opens into the courtyard. The kitchen was stark and eerie from the outside light. The straight-backed wooden chairs and a slab of table looked desolate and forboding. The kitchen is not like any other room when uninhabited. Geometric forms of cold steel and long knives out of the way of children hung where family portraits or gentle landscapes would in other rooms. Rugs did not break up the long wooden floor. My feet looked pale and far away. I must be getting taller and more Anglo again, I thought. My hands were very white. There was not a sound.

I put my face up to the back door and looked to the left to see that there were no lights on in the den where Frederico should have been comatose. I had initially thought of going out through the courtyard to the den but the doors, although

never kept locked, are old and squeaky. I took a deep breath.
I composed myself. I started to walk back out to the hall when
I heard footsteps coming from the stairs. I flattened myself
against the wall. This is not right, I thought. You must move.
You must go to the refrigerator and casually pour yourself a
glass of milk. You must not look like you are hiding or guilty
or like a ghost in a red shroud crucified to the white wall. You
must move, I told myself. I could not move. I could not breathe.
I could have even been dead except that my heart was beating
so fast. The footsteps continued. But there was something wrong
about them. Perhaps just a screen rattling in the wind. But
there was no wind. The sound was very close. It was almost
not human.

"Pepe!" I gasped as the old dog poked his head around
the corner. "What are you doing?"

I did not think the old dog was capable of such a flurry
of activity. His tail curled up and almost wagged. He gave a
short little whine. I unglued myself from the wall.

"Don't bark, Pepe. Please. What do you want? I'll give
you anything you want—food, water? Do you want to go out?
Just please don't bark."

He whined again.

"Pepe, look, here's some food."

He wouldn't look.

"And look, water."

He didn't move.

"Here is some nice milk, Pepe. Do dogs like milk?"

I opened the refrigerator and poured him a bowl.

Nothing.

I opened the back door gently. "You want to go out, good
dog?"

Nothing.

"Move it!" I said in the tone Rosa used when she ordered
him out. He moved it. I shut the door. It squeaked loudly. I

waited. There was still no other sound in the house. I took a dish towel in case Federico bled. I hoped there would be no blood. I moved quickly to the den.

I rapped lightly. There was no answer. I closed the door behind me. I went to close the heavy sliding glass door over the screen, but it squeaked too loudly, so I left it open and closed the drapes. If he did scream, he would wake up the whole house even if the glass door was closed. But he would not scream, I hoped.

I turned on the desk lamp, adjusted it to dim, and placed it on the floor behind the chair. Federico was heavy with drugged sleep. His face was still and sensuous against the white sheets. He would be worth reminding.

I sat on the couch where he slept.

"Federico, Federico!"

There was no answer.

"Federico, are you awake?" I asked in Spanish and English. I nudged him. I picked up his arm and let it drop. I opened his eyelid and it dropped back. I picked up his leg and it dropped. I shook him hard by the shoulders. I stuck my finger in his ear. Nothing. Nothing. But he was still alive. I could hear him breathing.

I pulled his jockeys off under the sheet. I spread his legs and tucked the towel beneath him still praying that there would be no blood. I would put the underpants back on when I had finished with a note inside them: "From your *wife.*" I went to the desk to write the note. I was not scared anymore. My heart still beat fast but with purpose, not fright. He would never tell anyone. He would never say, see how I limp, see this scar on my ball, I found it in my jockey shorts one morning with a note from my wife.

I took the paring knife out. It was small but sharp. With my back to the door, I knelt down. I tried to maneuver beneath the sheets, but it was too clumsy. I pulled the sheet down to his hips and there it was. All this trouble, I thought. All this goddamn trouble over this thing. I pinched his ball to make sure he was still out. Nothing. I held the cock up and selected the left side ball, the same side his father limps on, the same reminder. The light was not perfect but good enough. His cock sat like a soft fist on top of his balls. I held it up with one hand but found the flesh on his ball was too loose unless I held the skin tight with the other hand, which left me no hands for the knife unless I wanted to cut the whole thing off. But no, no. Just a thin scar up on top where he would see it to remind him. I held the bottom flesh taut with my left hand and held the knife firmly with my right. But that stupid cock kept flapping down in my way. This was not the way the details had presented themselves beforehand. Calm, you must remain calm, I said to myself. These problems were unforeseen, but not impossible, I said. If I could only get it to get hard so it would stay up and out of the way and maybe tighten up the slack on his ball too. I checked his face which remained heavy with sleep. I played with his cock in my hand. Nothing. I pumped it hard up and down. Nothing. My hand began to ache. You bastard, I thought. I have seen you pull this one before and it's only when you want one thing. I put my mouth over his cock and licked and sucked until my cheeks were about to cave in. I felt something stir. I sucked harder. It rose quickly.

"Ummm," I heard him gently murmur. I quickly looked at his face. It had not changed. I pinched his balls hard. Nothing.

"Ummm," he murmured again when I sucked.

Let them write this phenomenon in the medical journals, I thought. The cock stayed straight up and hard. I held the ball taut with the knife firmly in my other hand. I had practiced this move with an orange from my breakfast tray. I moved quickly.

"Oooooo!" I screamed.

The dog was barking in the room. Inside the room! A thin strong hand covered my mouth. I was pulled down on the floor behind the couch.

"Oooooo!" I tried to scream but the hand tore into my mouth from behind. The light was knocked over and broke. The dog barked furiously in the darkness.

"Don't move and don't scream," a firm voice whispered in my ear. I didn't move. I didn't scream. The hand stayed over my mouth but not as hard.

I heard a deep drunken voice singing from outside the front of the house: "*Ay, ay, ay, ay. Canta y no llores...*"

The dog stopped barking and began to howl from the other side of the room. Footsteps and a light in the hall.

"No, it is just my husband and the dog, Papa. I have it."

It was Rosa's voice and there was joy in it. She opened the door to the den and the dog stopped howling and ran out.

Juan Ortega must have been very drunk, "*Ese lunar que tienes cielito lindo,...*" he sang.

I heard Rosa shushing him. It sounded like she was practically carrying him. Her joyous voice droned on, "My poor little one. Shush now. Mama will help you. Mama will help you, Baby. Shush now. Mama will help now that you are home where you belong."

Jesus Christ, it was disgusting. Then I remembered the hand over my mouth. It smelled like flower water and rubbing alcohol. The Señora! I let out an involuntary gasp.

"Be quiet and stay down," the voice whispered in my ear.

Rosa must have heard us. She cracked open the door wider.

"It's OK, Federico. It's just Juan and me," she said.

Except that Federico didn't reply of course. The light shone right in on the couch behind which I was still pinned down by the Señora. The light from the wall illuminated Federico.

"Disgusting," Rosa said.

"What's disgusting?" Juan slurred.

"Cover him, please, Juan," she said.

Juan stumbled forward. It sounded as if Rosa had stopped his fall. A few more feet and they would have seen us behind the couch. They were very close.

"Never mind," Rosa said. "But why does he have a towel underneath it?"

Juan tried to laugh, but he had trouble managing little more than a grunt. "Shit, if he took my advice, he'd have a woman instead of a towel underneath it."

They left. The door clicked shut. The Señora (yes, there was no longer any doubt in my mind that it was the Señora and not an apparition) said in my ear, "I am going to take my hand away now. Don't scream and don't talk."

I was too frightened to scream. She took her hand away and we both sat up on the floor behind the couch.

"Is my son sick? Why doesn't he wake up?"

Tears were streaming down my cheeks. I was blubbering like an idiot. "No, no. He is only drugged."

"From what? Is he taking sleeping pills, too?"

"Yes, Abuela, yes. How did you?..."

"Shhh, I must get back. All this noise. Although this nurse tonight is the one who also takes my sleeping pills."

Tears burned my eyes. I didn't even know if I was seeing straight.

"What were you doing? Were you going to kill him?"

"No! No! Abuela."

"I didn't think so. But the dog was whining outside and I heard Juan singing and I had to hide quickly before the dog started barking. When I peeked through the curtain, I could only see your back, but from the shadows on the ceiling, I thought you had a big knife."

"No, no, Abuela, it wasn't a *big* knife."

"Oh, well what…well, I am sorry that I interrupted whatever you were doing, but I don't think it would have done much good, Rubia, the way he is sleeping. I must go back now. But whenever you see me from now on, don't scream. Do you understand? And I'd keep this between us or else they'll really think you are crazy. Do you understand?"

"Yes, yes."

"And tomorrow, come and see me no matter what they tell you. I have been looking everywhere for you for the past few days. Didn't you leave your bed? We must talk and you must bring me some of the medicine like today. Exactly like today, mix it. Do you understand?"

"Yes. Yes."

She went back out through the curtain into the courtyard. I crawled to the other side of the couch and stuck the knife, which had landed on the floor, back into my cuff. I sat on the floor until it began to get light. I put the broken lamp on the desk. Silently, I went back up to my room.

16

I am no longer a prisoner. I just don't have the time right now and it no longer interests me.

I did not think. I just sat at the desk when I got back to my room. It intrigued me how the light played. How the cold morning water from the faucet felt on my face. How the towel warmed my face. I dressed, feeling the sensations of each layer on my skin. I went to the girls' room and watched the light illuminate their sleeping faces. I did not wake them. I went down into the kitchen where Ada was just beginning her morning ritual. The smell of fresh coffee began to fill the morning. Her son, José, the stable boy who is no longer a boy, but a handsome young man, came in. On seeing me in the kitchen, or anywhere else I suppose at that early hour, he issued a look of surprise uncompromised by the limits of speech and hearing. He gave his mother a perfunctory kiss on the cheek. Ada gave him coffee and a fresh roll and hurried him to a chair at the table.

Señor Rodriguez came in. "How refreshed and different you look, Rubia. It looks like the effects of that long sleep have not worn off yet. Are you turning into an early bird after all these years or is something wrong?"

"No, Abuelo, there is nothing wrong, thank you."

Was it me speaking so politely and naturally when I had not been to sleep in a day? It was so easy on this new planet. Everything was different. Even more different than it had been, as if the whole planetary system had been moved to a different sun during the night. The order was the same. But the light was somehow different. The Señora was alive! I mean not only not dead but alive and strong. I had really seen her in the courtyard the night they had accused me of hallucinations. I was not crazy. I had felt her hand ripping into my mouth last night. What kind of power did she possess? What kind of power did I possess that could have evened up the score with Federico—my hand was already in motion and the knife only inches away when the Señora knocked me over. There was something big going on. Something powerful. Something on a new planet.

Had I been a prisoner of my own jealousy and tension while the old woman, my mother-in-law, my alter-ego from the old world, had slipped the constraining bonds of this house, of medical science, of terminal cancer? I was beginning to understand why they have upside-down question marks at the beginning of sentences in Spanish along with regular ones at the end.

Señor Rodriguez left with José. Rosa came in, ignored Ada and myself and prepared a tray (the same silver one that I had used the night before) with rolls and coffee. She announced that her husband was feeling a little "under the weather" so she would take him some food in case he felt up to eating.

"Fine," Ada said.

As Rosa was leaving with the tray she turned to me, "Just simple talk, woman to woman. A wife must do more than just bring coffee. A wife has other duties, no?"

It took a moment for her words to register as I considered the view of my husband as witnessed by Rosa the night before. Somewhere in the back of my head, an old voice, a voice I had possessed on another planet, almost said, "Go on, Rosa, go perform your wifely duties beyond bringing coffee. Go spread those sweet thighs to keep your husband between them instead of a towel or a tourist." But I kept silent and I started to laugh. And laugh. And laugh.

I was catching my breath when José and Señor Rodriguez returned.

"We could not get Federico out of bed. He kept mumbling about the ways of love and would not move," said Señor Rodriguez.

This made me start laughing all over again.

"What is so funny?" Señor Rodriguez asked me.

"Oh, no, I am sorry. It was only that Rosa had just told me a joke which was very funny."

"Rosa?" Rosa had never intentionally told a joke in her life.

"What I had to say was no joke and for Rubia's ears only and you can tell her I have proof," Rosa said.

"Ada, what was the joke?" Señor Rodriguez said.

"I do not know, Señor. I do not understand jokes. I only know that God moves in mysterious ways," Ada said.

"Abuelo, it was just a word joke. Please excuse me for seeming so rude."

"Yes, of course. But your husband wanted to come with us to check on some wood over on the north side and now I cannot wake him. I thought that was what you were laughing about."

"Maybe all that racket last night kept him awake, Papa? Maybe that is why he is so tired," Rosa said.

"Yes, I guess I'll let him sleep."

"What racket?" I couldn't help myself asking as if I didn't know.

"Oh nothing. My husband came home a little late, that's all," Rosa said.

"Rosa, I am glad for you," I said and meant it, surprising myself.

"Look, Rubia," said Rosa angrily, bending over my ear so

close that I could feel her sweat. "Your husband is really so tired because he had to use a towel last night because you are negligent of your duties." She stormed from the room with the silver tray.

I began to laugh again.

There were many things I should have done after breakfast. I should have gone into Saint and found out what Maria-Elena was doing as acting manager and if she knew that I knew. But no matter what was happening there, the three Spinning Marias would still be in the back making lace so there was no rush.

I should have gone to the lawyer or at least thought about getting a divorce, but on this planet, things did not have the same significance. Maybe the Señora was cured. Maybe she would not die.

I took a nap. I mixed the medicine earlier than usual. As per the Señora's instructions the night before, I tried to duplicate the way I had mixed it yesterday leaving out much of the morphine and going heavily on the cocaine and Ada's second cousin's cure. My curiosity got the better of me and I decided to bring the medicine up earlier than usual in the afternoon.

"Where are you going?" Rosa cut me off in the hall.

"To bring the medicine to your mother."

"You cannot do that. You are not allowed near my mother."

"I am no longer a prisoner, Rosa. I can go where I please."

"Not until the doctor, who thinks you are sick in the head, checks you out."

"Fine, have him check me out. But I am bringing this medicine now." I brushed her aside. She looked astonished.

"And the priest. I am going to have the priests check you out too!"

"Fine. You can bring on the entire Spanish Inquisition if you like."

It was the head of the visiting nurse service herself who

greeted me when I knocked on the Señora's door. Head Nurse Valencia is a dedicated, intelligent, no-nonsense person, not a person to put anything over on. My only hope was that she was not as familiar with the daily routine as the other nurses who were usually here. I decided on a direct approach.

"I have the Brinkston's Cocktail for the Señora," I said.

"You may put it on the table. Thank you. But aren't you a little early?"

"Yes, I am. But Doctor Garcia told me only to give it to her in the evening, not exactly at what time, and that it could only help to relieve not cure."

"That is correct. It is not a cure."

"So I had some time now so I made it early. The exact time is not important in your medical opinion either?"

"No, not in my opinion. It is just as well as I have your mother-in-law up now anyway."

"You are here inspecting then, Nurse Valencia?"

"No, we are short-handed, so I fill in where necessary. Thank you, I'll give it to her."

"Please let me give it to her. It is the only thing I am allowed to do for the Señora."

"Please understand that I usually encourage relatives to participate in the care of their family—the same reason that you prepare the medicine, which I am not even sure does her any good—but your sister-in-law has made it clear to me that she does not want you near her mother while you are under 'stress' as she put it."

"Yes, that is true that she suddenly does not like me near her mother, but you also know how she dismissed the nurse who knits and then acted like she had nothing to do with it and how she spoke to you on the phone and how she has started to wear a black dress when her mother is still very much alive and receiving excellent care from the doctors and nurses. Yes, we are all under some 'stress' as Rosa calls it. I am not asking you to leave only that I may do something for the Señora to help and to save you the trouble."

"Well go ahead. You know, we've had several nurses quit since we took on this case. Your sister-in-law is difficult sometimes. There are straws on the night table, I can help you if you need it."

Head Nurse Valencia sat back in the armchair and opened a magazine. Oh wise decision-maker! That is why she is in charge. But all this wise decision-making only to be allowed past the doorway. I would soon have to convince the doctors and priests and anyone else Rosa calls in to examine me that I am fine and should be allowed to visit the Señora at any time and by myself.

Shit, I almost said aloud after I had climbed over and around flowers, tables, fruit, plants, medicine and statues of various saints to get to the lace-canopied and lace-cushioned bed. Shit, the Señora had gone off again and the secret would be found out soon anyway. But my surprise at the empty bed was only momentary. She was propped up in the arm-chair on the other side of the bed. A sheet, tied across the front of the chair, held her in place. She had shrunk. An IV tube ran into her left hand which was held in place on the arm of the chair by a knotted towel. I quickly went around to the other side while balancing the cocktail tray on my arm. Nurse Valencia continued to read the magazine.

I put a straw in the drink and knelt by the chair to offer it to the Señora's pale mouth. I made light chattering noises to encourage her because the old sick woman looked like she needed soft cooing sounds and could not have been the wiry steel that held my mouth shut and my body prone the night before. There was no mystery. I made a mistake. I was under too much stress. My new planetary system quietly imploded.

"Abuela, please take a little. Ahhh, that's right. Sip a little more. This is food for you. Yes, yes, good medicine for you," I said sadly to the pale little doll.

A tiny breathless voice from her cracked lips whispered between my chatter: "Good cover, Rubia. Keep talking...come tonight...medicine, IV out at nine. Nurse is on...who takes sleeping pills...come after, we'll talk."

She knew what she was talking about. I had not made any mistake, but only that she had shrunk so. She sipped. I kept chattering. Slowly, slowly, the breathless words came and the glass emptied and the voice was silent. Her head dropped a little as if to sleep. I took the tray with me to the door.

"Thank you, nurse. She is tired now. Thank you..."

I bathed and dressed for dinner. I wore a simple white shirt dress. I would be ready for this inquisition or any other inquisition to come.

I went down to the kitchen before dinner. I combed Patricia's hair and listened to Margherita's tales of new nuns and new classes. One of Margherita's good sisters apparently told the class that all one had to do to become a nun was to have a vocation and all one had to do to have a vocation was pray. Margherita was very excited about this. I smiled and inwardly vowed to buy Margherita a bra, even if she didn't need one, to get her mind off convents. Dear Jesus, I prayed, may she at least get her period before the nuns sweep her away. In the face of my idle and chattering daughters, Rosa's three girls were dutifully polishing the good silver because there would be company for dinner. Rosa was angry, because, Ada told me quietly, Doctor Garcia did not think it was an emergency to come and examine my state of mind and told Rosa to schedule an appointment with the office.

Father Miguel, the head of the parish, also did not think it was an emergency that I had brought prescribed medication up to the Señora with the nurse there. But he did acquiesce to send one of the parish priests over at Rosa's insistence.

"Which one is coming Ada?" I asked.

"Father Tomaso."

"Which one is he? Do I know him? Has he ever been here before?"

"No, he is the one who sells the mass cards in the rectory. You might not know him but you have seen him—he's kind of old and skinny but with a little stomach, grey hair with a little bald spot."

"Oh, yes. I can remember him now." But I could not think of anything more about him except that he looked like an elderly clerk when I had accompanied the Señora to the rectory to buy mass cards on various occasions.

Rosa was busy supervising and had sent everyone but me into the den to get Federico moving. She was able to wake him but could not get him past his right sock. Dinner finally started without him in the formal dining room.

"My brother," Rosa explained to Father Tomaso, "is not feeling well, but hopefully will join us shortly. Please excuse him."

Father Tomaso looked ill-at-ease. He was not one of the usual parish ambassadors and probably would look ill-at-ease anywhere outside of the rectory. He only looked up from his plate when Ada, who probably bought more mass cards than anyone else, cleared his dish or placed another before him. The girls were respectfully quiet. Señor Rodriguez played with his food. Rosa talked incessantly about nothing in particular and shot me occasional glares. Juan Ortega, even in his freshly pressed embroidered shirt, looked like the walking dead and only drank the wine. I answered when spoken to. I silently sympathized with the old priest and in his presence I had renewed faith in the Church and medical science that neither had declared my inquisition a state of emergency. Besides, the roast Ada served was delicious and I was very hungry. The table was cleared and the girls hustled off. Coffee was served.

"Again, Father Tomaso, you must please excuse my brother

for not being here," Rosa repeated for the tenth time. Father Tomaso began to get fidgety.

"But we may begin without him," Rosa continued. "My sister-in-law has been acting very strange."

"Oh?" said Father Tomaso, looking at me.

"Well, what I mean," Rosa said, "is that my sister-in-law said that my mother, who is dying as you know, appeared to her in a vision and a few days after that she was found locked in my mother's room sleeping on the same bed with my dying mother. I am going to have a phone installed...a white one...and I think it would be better if she did not see my mother as she did this afternoon."

The old priest still did not seem to comprehend why or what type of slaughter he was being led to. I didn't think it was my place to assist Rosa in damning me and I looked mutely at her to continue.

"What I mean, Father, is that after such behavior, I do not think she is competent to see my mother who is very ill and I thought you might agree."

"I don't know how I can help, Señora Ortega." He was grasping for his coffee spoon.

I knew I should have kept my mouth shut and let Rosa damn herself, but I began to feel sorry for the priest.

"Father Tomaso, please understand that there were reasons for my behavior and that Doctor Garcia will give me a thorough examination in his office. You must excuse us for burdening you with our stressful situation."

Ada calmly served cake. The priest began to eat the chocolate cake with obvious relief that the matter had drawn to a close. I followed suit. The cake was excellent.

"Father, if you please, we await your decision," Rosa said when Father Tomaso was half through the piece of cake.

The cake suddenly didn't taste very good. I could not keep eating chocolate cake while an innocent old priest was being inquisitioned at my inquisition. I searched my mind for a change of subject but what does one talk about to old priests who work in the rectory? I couldn't very well ask him how the mass card business was doing. Rosa had already covered the weather during her main course chatter. God? Saints? Yes, I could switch the subjects to saints. I kept trying to remember what Saint Thomas had done that made him a saint but "doubting Thomas" was all I could remember.

"I'm sorry. I don't understand what you want me to decide," Father Tomaso said.

"If my sister-in-law should be allowed in my mother's room, Father."

The old priest appeared confused, but perhaps it was Rosa's threatening tone which enabled him to pull together the forces he might have needed to deal with an occasional irate mass card purchaser.

"Señora Ortega, if you please, Doctor Garcia must be more familiar with the situation and could put these details into perspective. Perhaps now we should only pray for guidance to the right path."

"I can give you all the details necessary, Father," Rosa said.

"I think the good father is right, Rosa," Señor Rodriguez said. "Let him finish his cake now."

But Father Tomaso didn't look like he was still in the mood for chocolate cake. An uneasy silence prevailed. I finally remembered what Saint Thomas did.

"Father," I blurted out. "I have often thought that it must have been easy for your patron saint, Saint Thomas, to believe. If God sent a lightning bolt to throw me from my horse and spoke to me from heaven, I would surely be a saint now."

"Rubia!" Rosa scolded.

"Señora Rodriguez," Father Tomaso said and smiled for the first time, "I think it was Saint Paul who was thrown from his horse and heard God's voice from the heavens."

"Oh, I'm sorry."

"Saint Thomas was the one called 'doubting Thomas.' He did not believe that Christ had died and had risen so the Lord appeared to him after the resurrection and made him put his hands into his wounds and he then believed."

"Oh, of course. Excuse me...I was confused for a moment."

"Only by the name perhaps. Perhaps we all would be saints too if Jesus appeared to us and made us put our hands in his wounds."

"Aren't there any saints who were saints because they were just holy even without being sent such magnificent signs from God? Weren't some of the saints just able to believe?"

"I think there were many like that who knew that there are miracles all around us in everyday life, only perhaps Saint Paul and Saint Thomas needed the more spectacular to believe, so God allowed them the spectacular."

Father Tomaso stopped. I think that if he gave the sermons on Sunday, I might go to church more often even if his voice was old and frail. I had thought that the priest was finished or only pausing for thought when I saw the real reason he stopped speaking. Silence filled the room. It was Federico. He had appeared. He was impeccably dressed for dinner with the exception of one shoe, which he held in his hand. He looked unsteady, and not only because he only had one shoe on, but resolute in purpose like a drunk headed for a bottle. In fact, I thought he was headed for the bottle of after-dinner brandy on the table.

Rosa was covering poorly. "Federico, you are feeling better and have joined us at last."

Federico was directly behind me. He lifted the pageboy off my neck in one sweep and passionately kissed the back of my neck.

"*Mi amor!*" he said.

"Federico!" Rosa said.

"Jesus Christ, Federico, what are you doing?" I said.

Juan Ortega began to laugh.

"She is my wife, Father. We are blessed." And started to kiss my neck again. He dropped the shoe from his hand.

Rosa must have made apologies to the good priest as she rushed him to the door.

One on each side, Señor Rodriquez and I dragged Federico back to the den.

"How did you get so drunk?" his father asked.

"No," the drugged voice answered. "Papa, I am in love only and not drunk. She is wonderful, no?...wonderful."

"Yes, she is. Now walk, my son."

Federico was still dribbling in the top of my hair. Not exactly the effect I was looking for, I thought, as Federico's heavy shoulder brought me out from my mystical connection with the old priest. Not the scrotal scar I had envisioned when I mixed the morphine into the coffee the previous night. I had almost forgotten about Federico under the spell of Saint Paul and/or Thomas. Why couldn't Federico just have slept peacefully and then woke up missing a day or two like I had under the influence? And why all the goddamn saliva? My mouth had been like cotton when I woke up.

We had him flat on the couch. Well, almost flat. A telltale bulge in his pants looked like a tent. Señor Rodriguez unlaced his son's one shoe. Rosa brought the other shoe in. Ada followed, apologizing—"I only gave him a little, Rosa. I made him drink just one glass of whiskey to get him moving. You told me to get him moving. I never suspected one glass of whiskey, or maybe two, would get him like this. My God, what the poor old priest must think. I never thought..."

"*Mi amor!*" Federico kept grabbing for me.

"Ah, how sweet," Ada said. "All he talked about was you, Rubia. He still loves you like a newlywed."

"This is your fault, Rubia," Rosa spat in my ear. "To make such a sacrilege in front of the priest. Even the Catholic Church doesn't allow wives to starve their husbands to have to use a towel."

Federico seemed to have fallen asleep.

"Leave them alone. Rubia can take care of this I think," my father-in-law said and moved them out and shut the door.

"Ah. Ah, I tricked you, *mi amor*," Federico said and tried to wink. He was holding me or trying to.

"Fuck off, Federico," I told him in English.

His voice was that of a drunk. "You will never be a lady with that dirty mouth, but that makes it more delicious, my passion," he answered in Spanish. "Come on now. I know all about last night, my passion. My little passion."

I nearly jumped off the couch. "Now take your hands away and tell me all about last night, Federico."

"How about you showing me again and I'll tell you if it's right."

"No." Firmly. "You tell me."

The voice was thick: "I thought it was a dream, *mi amor*, how you came to me in the night with your hands and your mouth and then I thought that I dreamt someone was singing. Everything was so strange and romantic. There was a candle, but it went out and you were gone. All a dream I thought...but today, I found the towel you had placed beneath me last night...but don't worry, *mi amor*. I hid the towel. And then when Ada came in, I was very tired, and she asked me why the lamp was broken. Ah, ah. I thought, the candle that went out. I have evidence like a detective, but don't worry, it is only our secret that you could not stay away. It was a beautiful dream, but more beautiful now that I know it is true. You could not stay away and you tried to hide it from me...."

Damn, he was falling asleep.

"Is that all, Federico?"

"That is enough, my passion."

I shook his shoulders "Are you sure that is all?"

"All that matters. But if you want more I will tell you that no one else ever really mattered and we will go together to tell Maria-Elena that. She was never anything to me like you are...she was only for comfort, not for real. If you do not believe me, then yes, you can come with me when I tell her that it is all over between us."

I was too stunned to move. It was true. Oh, I knew it. I knew it a thousand times, but it was a different kind of pain to actually hear the words of truth from his mouth. Federico slept. I did not wake him. I was very sad. There were no ball-cutting tears of rage. Only sadness.

A hand knocked on the door. "Is everything all right, Rubia?"

"Yes, Abuelo. Thank you."

I waited until his footsteps died away. Then I went upstairs to my room.

17

≈ ≈ ≈ ≈ ≈ ≈ ≈ ≈ ≈ ≈ ≈

I lay on the bed and watched the ceiling fan. I fell asleep. I dreamt of a huge concert hall where my sister was playing the piano to a packed house in tuxes and diamonds. I was on stage also, dancing a merengue in a bra and panties. Suddenly, there were no people and the sound of one person clapping echoed through the hall. I heard my mother's voice from the back of the hall, "Come on, girls, it's time." My sister and I giggled, "Oh please, Mom, let us play a little longer."

"No, you can do that later. It's time now." She clapped again and I awoke with a start. The clock on the night stand said 1:00 A.M. I went quickly to the Señora's room.

I have memorized every word, every gesture, every shadow that played that night. A night light cast my shadow on the wall. The nurse, as my mother-in-law had predicted, was sleeping in the chair by the door. The Señora sat in the same chair where I had left her. Except that there were no sheets holding her up. Except that this was not the shriveled doll that I had left. This was the Señora. Her back was straight, her hands folded in her lap.

"I thought you'd never come," she said. "I even went down to the courtyard to see if I could see you sitting at your desk. I peeked into the den to see if you were with Frederico, too. Ah, but look at you, Rubia, your face is so sad."

"Yes," I said and looked back at the sleeping nurse.

"Oh, don't worry about her. She's slept through worse commotions than this. She even slept through Juan Ortega's singing last night. But come, if you'd be more comfortable, we can talk in the other room."

We moved through the passage to the little sitting room overlooking the courtyard. Through the door, a flight of outside steps led to the rose garden.

"Well, do I look dead?"

"No, Abuela, you look wonderful. How did it happen that you are cured?"

Every shadow...her dark eyes shone. Her skin was soft and lined. The high cheek bones. The black hair frosted with silver flowed down her back. The white gown I had bought for her. Her command. Her power. Her hands gestured as she spoke.

"Sit down, Rubia. We have much to talk about."

"May I hug you first, Abuela?"

"Yes, of course, you must touch me to see if I am real, no?"

But no, that was not the reason. Here they touched and hugged more than we did at home, but much of it was ritualistic. I needed to hug with affection; my own mother was still close from my dream.

She was strong when I hugged her. We sat to the side of the window in the shadows.

"Abuela, how has this happened? Why haven't you told anyone that you are cured?"

"Wait now, Rubia. You must ask one question at a time. It is not a cure. It is from the medicine, the cocktail as you call it. But only sometimes. Sometimes it just takes away the pain and sometimes it makes me feel nice and other times, I feel wonderful, like I should never have been in bed at all, like now. I presume that it is not prepared in the same way."

"No, the doctor told me to mix it according to how you

seem each day and the doctor allows me to add some of the local cures as they are brought."

"Well from now on, you must prepare it the way you have been the past week or so. This has been the best."

"But you are cured. Why haven't you told anyone?"

"Cured? No, Rubia. Even the doctor has told you it is not a cure. Even when I feel wonderful, the disease is always, always with me. Sometimes, in the morning, it is like a wolf waiting to finish off its stalked prey. But when I feel good from the medicine at night, it feels only like an old dog, like Pepe underfoot. But the disease is always with me, Rubia, it does not go away."

"Why didn't you tell us, why didn't you..."

"Always, you have been the impatient one. Like your children. In some ways, they are much like you.

"The cocktails were not served until I had been home a few days, am I correct? And then it did not happen all at once. At first I felt only a little better and then I felt good and then I felt like dancing. It had been so long since I had felt any energy; it scared me. And I had heard that when a person is very sick that they always receive a surge of energy right before they die so that is what I thought was happening. I was scared. I only used my new energy to pray, but again and again death did not come. So I became more bold. But it was only at night after the medicine. I got out of bed and they put me back in. I spoke like a convert of my new energy and they gave me tranquilizers for my delirium. Finally, I ripped out IV's and tubes, overturned tables from anger to show how strong I had become. That was when they started to tie me down with the sheets and towels. My own sheets! And in the mornings, I am always so exhausted anyway. I had to change my tactics to get the restraints off. I became a 'good' patient. And as I said, I do not feel so good every night. I learned not to upset anyone and I learned the habits of the different nurses—this is not the first string of nurses you know. The ones who didn't quit because of my tantrums quit because of Rosa's. This one, who is fairly new, takes one of my pills and sleeps through anything. I tried to get your attention several times at night. You were the only one who really talked to me when you came to visit, so I thought you still might think me capable of existence outside the vegetable world. Also, you are the only one who stays up late at night."

She laughed. "I couldn't very well knock on your door. But what a racket you put up when you finally saw me—screaming and yelling about ghosts, and you always accused Latins of dramatics. I barely had time to climb the steps to the room and get into bed. Of course, after that, you were forbidden to come. But that does not matter. You are here now."

"Abuela, it is a miracle. It is magic."

"No. Only perhaps a gift from God to a dying woman trying to put things in order before she dies."

But no, it was a miracle. It was magic. Every gesture, every shadow lay in its spell. I felt as beautiful and magical as the woman I looked on in the shadows. It was the kind of beauty that does not fade with age, something female and strong, something that comes from being a part of magic.

"Now, Rubia, you must not sit there looking so...unwell. Sadness becomes some women; on you it looks ugly. Now you must tell me at once why you look so sad. These nights are not as long as I would like them to be."

"Abuela, it is not important. We must figure out a way to get you feeling like this all the time to make them believe."

"I have already tried, my stubborn one. You were not my first choice to reveal my new energy to. As far as medical science and the rest of my family is concerned, I am already a dead woman. We fall back on custom and tradition here when there is a crisis. Do you think if we both went right now and told them how well I feel at night and what things I am capable of after the medicine that they would sit calmly and listen to you, whom they think hysterical, or to me, an old sick woman who has already received the last sacrament three times? No, Rubia, it would not work like that. And if you tell them what you are seeing, they will never, never let you up here again. And besides, I have told you, I must sleep sometime so I sleep through most of the morning. I am not in pain, only exhausted. It is a fine line, I heard Doctor Garcia say, between how much medication will kill the pain and how much will kill the patient. It is enough to be awake and about at night. It makes the night easier and the nights have been the hardest time since I have been ill. One's childhood fear of the darkness comes back when you are old and dying perhaps. Years ago, I had hoped to die old and peacefully during the night—just not get up in the morning. When I first got sick and was in the hospital, each night when I closed my eyes that silly wish came to mind. It would keep me awake all night. Now I wish only to die in the daytime, with the sun in the window, so that I will move into the light.... Ah, so like a sick old woman to ramble on so. It is important for me to know why you are looking so sad. I need you to stay here now. I never suspected that you would think of leaving now."

"Abuela, I would not think of leaving while you are so sick."

"Yes, you have finally learned to be a good Spanish daughter and would wait until I die. But I already have a good Spanish daughter, Rubia. If you have to go, then go now. I need you here after I die. I have thought it all over. You will be in charge when I die. So I have explained my mystery and now you must talk to me about your plans for leaving or staying."

"Abuela, when I sneaked up here to you last week, I told you about Frederico. It was in the afternoon. You were your 'other self.' I mean that you were exhausted. But you must remember if you know that I was thinking of leaving. It was only that Frederico and I were having some mistaken marital problems and I had been a little sad about that. But it is not important, not important at all and all these problems have been taken care of."

"Don't lie to me. If it is a day or a year that I have left, it is not enough time for lies. And don't talk like a martyr. It looks worse on you than sadness. It's late in life for you to start to cultivate that useless virtue. My mother-in-law was a martyr. My own daughter is a martyr. I am not a martyr and neither are you. That was initially the only reason I spent so much time and effort with you when you came here as a foreigner. Not because you were my daughter-in-law and not because you were dutiful, you were anything but. My own daughter is far more dutiful than you will ever be, but she is a martyr. You were like an avenging princess when you came here. You despised our 'slave system' as you called it, but you enjoyed breakfast served to you in bed. But at least, you were not a martyr. Do you understand?"

"Yes, Señora Rodriguez, I understand."

"Yes, you do. Your disrepect creeps back into your voice. But I have always preferred that to humility."

I smiled. I wondered how the nurses could have ever thought her delirious.

"Rubia, I remember well that afternoon. You said that Frederico was having an affair with Maria-Elena. She is that girl who manages your store, no? And that you wanted to leave him and go home. It upset me very much, but I was my 'other self' as you say, and I was very exhausted. I was not much help to you at the time, I'm afraid. I believe I told you to even the score."

"You told me to cut off his balls. You told me that you had cut off your husband's balls and that that is why he limps."

She laughed. "Yes, I believe I did say something like that. I was very angry at my son to do something to drive you away after so many years. My son is not usually a fool. Ah, Rubia, it is wonderful to be an old 'disoriented' woman and finally be allowed to use whatever language one cares to use. It is nice to be so unlimited. Sometimes I mutter marvelous improper words under my breath to the nurses who bother me. At least with you I can say them out loud. You always had a bad mouth. I remember when you first came, you would call me 'your highness' in English everytime I instructed you harshly. I asked Rosa what it meant and she looked it up and told me that it was a very reverent form of address in English only used for royalty—a high compliment to you, she told me. Oh, how I laughed right in front of her! Well, Rubia, did you cut off his balls and even it up yet?"

"No, Abuela, but I almost..."

"My God, then you did have a big knife in your hand last night. I saw a shadow on the ceiling. Mother of God!"

"No, no, it was only small, like a nail file. It was a nail file—I just wanted to give him a scratch."

"God must have sent Juan Ortega home drunk and Pepe barking and me into the nearest place to hide at that instant to stop you, Rubia. God must have forgiven me after all these years for how I avenged my husband by allowing me to stop you at that instant. There's one sin off my mind now that I am dying, thank God for his mercy."

"Then you did cut off Abuelo's balls!"

"Rubia, you sound so young sometimes. I had not thought of talking about this now. I had not thought of talking about it at all. It must be further penance for my sins, which at least I know are forgiven now."

"Abuela, you needn't tell me."

"No, you have a right to be curious now. I have so much else to discuss with you yet, maybe it will help to tell you. Only you must promise that you will not leave here until we have talked again and that you will not do anything, anything else crazy to Federico. He is still my son even though I am angry at him. And you must not think of leaving here either until we have discussed so much more. You must promise me that."

"Abuela, I promise you."

"You must understand that when I first came here, I was very young. Seventeen to be exact. Not so young maybe by today's standards but I was very naive. I came from here, as you know. But the part of Saint I grew up in was very different from the hacienda. The big houses in the old part of town were very grand but many very poor. My father, like so many others, had gambled high stakes during the rubber boom and lost. He lived on credit and liquor after that. My mother lived on illness and God. God bless her. My only sister had married a wealthy Argentinian and went to live in Buenos Aires when I was ten. My mother's only concern was to get a proper husband for me before our creditors caught up with us. Our parents and Federico's parents had known each other for many years. I had known Federico since he was a boy through my father's business and through church, of course. By the time I took serious notice of him, he was so independent; his father had died three years before and he was already in charge of his household. And very handsome. I thought myself the belle of the ball, having had my mother's preening and marriage preparations all to myself since a young age. Having one's virginity so protected and one's 'desirability' so advertised, one firmly came to believe oneself to be a priceless and rare gem.

"Federico and I had been on only five heavily chaperoned dates before he asked my father for my hand in marriage. As for my actual marriage preparation, my mother told me the night before the wedding, 'Margherita, even if you have heard some talk, you will be very surprised on your wedding night. Just lie very still and let him do what he has to do. Act pleased also for it is very necessary in a marriage and a woman needs to have babies, too.'

"My marriage was better than I expected. Even my wedding night was not so bad—Federico was very gentle. Federico's mother was basically a jolly, frivolous woman content to stay in widowed mourning as long as it didn't interfere with her social events. She was more than glad that her son, an only child and always too serious, she told me, had married and that I was here to help her. She let me do more than just help. She was happy for me to do everything and I did. I was also dedicated to helping Federico. I ran the house and soon did most of the bookkeeping for the hacienda.

"I enjoyed my status and I was deeply in love with my husband. I was very fascinated by the power my... sex had over him. It was not at all as my mother had described. To make a man tremble so by doing so little! And by doing so little more than what my mother had told me to, it seemed I could hold his very soul.

"All went well for two years except that I was not pregnant. This worried our parents more than it did me. For us, it only served to increase our *amors* with new purpose."

She breathed a deep sigh.

"Then came the war. Not even a real war but the usual every-twenty-year military overthrow of the government in the capital. It was new to us though. But it seemed so far away, separated by mountains and thousands of miles and we were even more isolated in that time. There was never any fighting here. There were newspaper headlines and what sounded like election year talk. But Federico thought of nothing else. His father had fought in a previous overthrow some thirty or forty years back. Federico devoured the newspaper, ignored my existence and spent most of his days in town talking politics. I could not understand his interest. I could not understand why he was abandoning me for something happening on another planet as far as I was concerned.

"My mother-in-law, who also did not understand politics, would only say, 'Yes, Federico, your father was a brave soldier when he fought.'

"Federico longed desperately to fight, 'for honor,' he said.

"'Federico, you already have honor,' I said. 'Why would you have to go somewhere to fight for it?'

"'Silly girl,' he would call me.

"We argued constantly.

"Oh yes, there was a woman, Maritza. She was from the capital. Her father had sent her here to live with her aunt while the fighting was going on. She sat in the cafes with the men. They thought she was a goddess, a political storehouse. She was pretty, fair with blue eyes and brown curly hair, very European-looking. Her father and two brothers were fighting, so every letter she got from home was discussed like a battle plan even though the letters sometimes took up to a month to reach her. Federico spoke of her constantly. Until one night, for the first time, he did not come home all night. He said he had been 'talking politics' with the boys all night in town. He never mentioned her name again in the house. I think that is how I first knew. Afterwards, he was not so very discreet. Even after he had left to go fight, I heard more news of him through others who had heard it from his letters to her than I did from his infrequent and brief letters addressed to his mother and myself.

"... maybe I drove him away, I was so angry about Maritza and the war. All he could talk about was the war.

"'Fine,' I spat at him, 'if it will make you more of a man, which you are not now, then go fight.'

"Almost eighteen months he was gone, Rubia. My tears dried the day he left. The hacienda would have probably run itself for that length of time. And he left his cousin Mario who was also his best friend to 'help' me. But I needed more than 'tea-socials' to channel my anger. I kept Mario as manager of

the stables where he was happiest anyway and I went to work.
I already had a two-year foundation from helping Federico.
I studied hard and worked hard. I took over everything shortly—
all the books, the purchase orders, the bargaining and selling,
the managing and directing. I was not afraid to get my hands
dirty. I had good common sense and also good intuition. I did
well. I discreetly paid my family's creditors.

"You came here talking of fairness and justice and slavery.
You have never seen slavery and poverty like I saw it then. I
had no idea it could exist like that, right here on our own land.
You spoke of 'work agreements' as 'penal servitude.' Yes, it has
come down through tradition and custom that a payroll is not
used but goods and services are exchanged. But I changed
these work agreements to be at least equitable for all parties.

"I also raised the living conditions of the people living in
the little scattered villages on land owned by the hacienda.
Land which I hadn't even known belonged to the hacienda
previously. And I invested well and with those profits bought
more land and raised living conditions there. And you thought
you were the first reformer here. I'm sorry you had to learn
the hard way, Rubia. You did not really fail, you just went too
fast without knowing enough. It was easier for me. I already
knew the customs and traditions. But oh, how I am digressing
or avoiding the main subject.

"Federico had been gone about six months when we heard
through the channels which I knew led to Maritza that Federico had been hurt. It was minor, they all said, and asked
what we had heard which was nothing, of course. My mother-
in-law was frantic. I tried to reassure here that everyone had
said it was only minor and that we would have heard personally
if it had been anything more.

"'But I know him.' she told me. 'He is probably suffering
very much and only does not want to alarm us.'

"We had been living with an unspoken agreement: You

pretend you don't know about Maritza and I'll pretend I don't know about Maritza. But that night we had a huge argument after dinner with Maritza's name holding prominent place.

"'He is a man,' my mother-in-law said. 'And if you had realized this a long time ago and accepted the fact that he has a mistress we wouldn't now be getting information secondhand through his mistress. And if you were any kind of a good wife or daughter-in-law, you would justify your past mistakes and be down begging her in order to find out exactly how my son was injured.'

"'I will not do this,' I told her. 'If your son's injuries were anything more serious than we have heard, we would have been informed officially. And there is nothing we could do about them anyway.'

"'We would pray,' she told me.

"'We can pray now.'

"'We would at least know exactly what we are praying for and how hard to pray,' she said.

"How can you argue with this type of reasoning, Rubia? She was frantic. She told me that if I didn't go, then she would go and talk to Maritza. I went against my better judgment, arranging a meeting for the next day at one.

"It was a huge mistake. Maritza's aunt, who seemed totally oblivious of the situation, served tea and said how glad she was that her niece was finally meeting friends of her own age and social status. Her niece had always been too politically involved as far as she was concerned, she told me. I thought the old woman would never leave us alone. And she never did. Finally, I suggested that we go for a walk and her aunt declined due to the arthritis she had been discussing at length.

"We walked a bit in silence. We sat on the chairs in the garden patio. I had worked out my words and actions beforehand like a chess game. You see, divorce was unthinkable in those days. It could only come down to an emotional, and sometimes financial, power play between the mistress and the wife. Then maybe some type of compromise.

"We were surrounded by garden flowers and the afternoon sun. I began to scrutinize her every feature—my opening move—hoping to make her ill-at-ease before I began. I had planned on asking her only one question before I left: 'My mother-in-law and I have heard that my husband's injuries are very minor. However, is there anything more regarding these injuries which you have learned of from home' (how discreet I had planned on being!) 'that we should know about?' But I never had the opportunity to recite my question to which I would have been happy to receive either a yes or no answer. While I was still inspecting the curve of her mouth and the color of her eyes, Maritza said, 'We no longer have to keep up our pretenses, Señora Rodriguez. What is the real reason you have come to see me? If it is to try to separate Federico and me, do not waste your time. We love each other deeply and have more in common together than you do.'

"'No,' I said like a confused schoolgirl. 'It was only to find out for my mother-in-law the details of my husband's injuries. We have heard that they are very minor but...'

"'If you need details, all the details, I'm afraid that I could not show his letters or tell you his words which are private between him and me only.'

"'I am not asking you to. Only if they are as minor as we have been led to believe.'

"'His injuries perhaps to you are minor, but his bravery was that of a hero.'

"She went on to tell me that Federico's left shoulder had been grazed by a bullet, not wounding him deeply, by God's grace, she said, but how brave Federico was to have taken a bullet which might have been meant for the heart of a general or her father or her brother. By the end of her speech, Federico's quarter-inch wound had saved the entire army. Her eyes were misty and her body shook with patriotism. She spoke as if Federico's wounds had proven his love for her.

"I seduced Mario that night, in the stable. I had never thought of revenge in those terms or even that my putting so much energy into the running of the hacienda and doing such a better job of it than Federico or his father had done was a way to get back. But now I did. And I put much more energy into both tasks. I seduced Mario many times after that, anywhere we could secretly meet. I was not in love with him. He said that he was in love with me, but sex was at such a premium in those days, who knows if he really loved me. The force of my revenge, the force of our guilt, the secretness of our meetings was enough to turn our lovemaking into a fire greater than love. Six months later, with tears streaming down his face, Mario told me that he could no longer love me while his best friend, his cousin, was patriotically fighting for honor and freedom and that he was going to join the fight also. I did not cry when he left either.

"The fighting was over soon after he left. I did not even know if he had time to join in any battles. Maritza left. It was months after that when Federico returned. Mario never returned.

"My husband's scar on his shoulder was indeed barely noticeable. But he had a fresher and much larger scar on his thigh and he limped severely. He told the story only once saying that it had happened during one of the last battles where Mario had died bravely fighting.

"I cried that night, the first time in eighteen months. I begged Federico to let me confess to him. I told him that I hadn't thought it would end this way and that I had to tell him why Mario had gone to fight also. But he would not grant me my confession. He would not let me say a word about it, 'now or ever,' he said. He made love to me silently. His body shook but not with the love we had known. It was with an absoluteness, a possession, that I had never known before.

"I have never regretted my actions, Rubia, although I will be forever sad that Mario did not return. He was so young and sweet. But maybe if I hadn't seduced him he would have gone to fight sooner and if it was God's will, would have died sooner. And yet, all those years I never got pregnant, I felt as if God was punishing me. I finally got pregnant twelve years later. I felt that God was finally taking my punishment away. And now he permitted me to stop you from giving my son a limp too. I am dramatizing, no?—you said all you were going to give him was a scratch. There are better ways to get back, Rubia. It is getting late and I am tired from having the medicine earlier than usual. It is wearing off too soon. Tomorrow we will start where I wanted to, Rubia, when you come back."

I helped her back through the adjoining room and back into bed. She was weaker now and slumping over—shrinking back into her other self. I kissed her forehead and left past the snoring nurse.

18

≈ ≈ ≈ ≈ ≈ ≈ ≈ ≈ ≈ ≈ ≈

O ne could never go insane here because there is always a brighter insanity lurking in the shadows to take you away. Federico opened the curtains. The gray light poured in. I only had about four hours sleep. I could have used about twelve.

"Rosa has arranged an appointment for you with Doctor Garcia for ten this morning, *mi amor*. But do not worry. I will go with you and I will tell him how I caused your insanity through my lapse. I will let no one forbid you to see my mother."

I do not like to be angered in the morning. I do not like to think in the morning. It is all I can do in the morning to coordinate my speech patterns into words such as, "Yes, I'll have a roll, please." The decisions I must make in the morning, I make. I put my underwear on before my dress instead of over it. I put Patricia's hair into a pony tail rather than complicating it into braids. I like to drink a lot of coffee in the morning.

"No! Federico. Get out of here."

"Yes, I understand. I will have your coffee waiting for you downstairs."

I put my clothes on. I had promised to see Doctor Garcia. It was only that I would have made the appointment for later in the day. It was only that Federico didn't think I was even capable of having my own insanity apart from him.

It was only that Federico called his making my assistant

manager his mistress a "lapse." He did not realize how his "lapse" had hurt me if he really still thought I went to the den two nights before to give him a blow job.

It was also the delicate balance of morning which should never be upset by things which happen in the night.

"Federico is down with José to bring the jeep around for you, Rubia," Ada said. "Would you care for more coffee?"

"Yes, thank you, Ada."

"Don't look so nervous, Rubia," she whispered. "The priest has already OK'd your mind and if Doctor Garcia OK's you too, then God will surely allow you more visions."

Doctor Garcia's waiting room looks more like a well furnished den than an aseptic anteroom. The couches are leather and plush. The drapes are heavy. The air-conditioning is blessedly cold. On the couch with me was a woman and two small children, well-behaved and well-dressed. I imagine most of the children seen by Doctor Garcia are well-behaved and well-dressed. Across from me was an elderly couple. The woman knitted. The man stared into space. Next to them sat, ah, Federico. I was not speaking to him. We had a heated debate in front of the house over his insistence on coming with me. José, in his unhearing sixth sense, took it all quietly in. Finally, I drove myself only to find Federico not far behind in one of the jeeps.

"Señora Roderiguez, the doctor will see you now," the nurse said. "Oh, Señor Roderiguez, I didn't see you. You may accompany your wife, of course."

"He doesn't need to be seen," I said. And the door closed behind me as Federico was just getting out of his chair.

For an hour before I saw the doctor, my height and weight were noted, my blood drawn, my urine taken, my electrocardiogram recorded. This was not the type of inquisition I had counted on. How could I convince an EKG machine that my heart was pounding so hard not from disease or insanity but because my husband was no good?

When Doctor Garcia finally saw me, I breathed deeply, coughed and said "ah" for him. He then inspected my ears, nose, throat, and vagina. But there was no secret insanity lurking in any of these places.

"You can dress now and go into my office."

In the office he said, "Rubia, I can find nothing wrong. Of course, we will not have the results of your blood or Pap test for several days. But I do not anticipate that these findings will be anything but normal also.

"Now tell me exactly what you say you saw in the courtyard that night that caused such a commotion."

"I saw the Señora, Doctor Garcia."

"I see. Tell me more."

"It was very pleasant, Doctor, not at all frightening the way everyone made it out to be. She was sitting at one of the tables very calmly with that way she has...well, you know the way she sits very upright but relaxed at the same time."

"Yes, go on."

"Well that's all except that she waved and when she did I screamed for some reason."

I thought the honest approach the best way. I had hopes of getting more medication for the Señora. It seemed the only way to rescue her from the grave before she died. I would have increased the dosage myself, but I had to find out from the doctor how much she could take without it killing her. I had to let him know that the Señora was responding well to the medicine.

"Doctor Garcia, if you please, what if I were to tell you that what I saw was real? That the cocktail medicine is miraculous?"

"Well, Rubia, I would tell you that many people have

illusions under stress. I see yours as a harmless illusion. As you describe, it appears as a wish fulfillment. But there is some conflict in the fact that you screamed. That you imagined you saw the Señora in very pleasant surroundings and that you saw her in no pain is a very positive sign as far as denial mechanisms go. If you had reacted better to the tranquilizers I had prescribed for you, then we would continue on that course of action. I am not worried that you had a bad reaction to them. It was an unusual reaction, but certainly not unheard of. Each person's system reacts differently to a drug, some more than others. But the fact remains that you did react badly to it which points to a different course of action. First of all, we should remove some of the stress: your care of your mother-in-law and also your preparation of the medicine. Indeed, I remember that caused you some anxiety from the first. I should have stopped it then.

"Secondly, I think that you should go and see one of my colleagues, a psychiatrist. It won't be as bad as you imagine. The nurse can make the appointment for you on your way out."

I must have been shrinking. I felt very small and lost. I thought that even if Doctor Garcia didn't believe me and if I was forbidden to see the Señora that I would just plan our midnight trysts more secretly, not that I would be forbidden to mix the medicine. Even if I could lie my way to sanity with the psychiatrist, how many days would be lost to the Señora if the medicine, which they were not convinced was really necessary, was to be discontinued or if someone else mixed it according to the old formula. I got up, dazed, tripped on my high heels and bumped into the wall.

"...unless of course we could be overlooking the obvious."

"What?" I answered and pulled my hand away from my bumped head in order to retain some semblance of dignity.

"Rubia, when was the last time you had your eyes checked?"

Holy shit. Why hadn't I thought of that? Thank you for

small miracles, Saint Thomas and/or Saint Paul.

"When I was a child I guess, sir." I tried to look especially gloomy to hold off the grin lurking in my heart. I put my hand back up to rub my head.

"Nurse, please come and check Señora Rodriguez's eyes."

I memorized the eye chart so I could approximate my performance if I was sent to the eye doctor. First with paper over one eye, then the other, then with both eyes, I followed the nurse's instructions.

"Read the third line up from the bottom, Señora Rodriguez."

"It's just a solid line," I told her feigning embarrassment.

"The fourth line from the bottom then."

"Oh, that's better. It's a row of dashes."

"Dashes?"

"Yes, dashes. Many little lines."

"And the next line?"

I phased out my eyes, like squinting without squinting, at the letters:

E O X M D G T O U

I said:

B G T N O O I G O

Line by line getting each letter wrong until the massive E was impossible to fake.

The nurse then made me come forward to the next yellow line of tape on the floor and do the same except that now I read the top two lines correctly. Then she had me move back and back until I was almost back into the examination room.

"I am sorry," I yelled to her. "I cannot even see the poster from here." In fact, even the nurse looked very tiny from there.

The nurse handed Doctor Garcia a folded sheet of paper.

Federico had sneaked in during my performance. Standing in the hall, Doctor Garcia continued speaking to him as he read the paper from the nurse. "Just as I thought, myopia. Just plain old-fashioned myopia."

They were both ignoring me, although I was standing right next to them.

"And all this talk about stress-induced illness. Ha! What clued me into the problem was when she said, 'It waved.' Now from that distance, a branch moving in the shadows could very well look like a waving figure to a myopic."

"Ah, Doctor, that is why when I followed her down here this morning—I knew something was wrong so I followed her in the jeep—she was all over the road. I had never driven behind her before—she was everywhere," Federico said.

I cleared my throat several times. I bumped into the wall on purpose.

"Yes, driving will be forbidden to her now until an optometrist has checked her and fitted her glasses. A myopic can see up close. She can read and the condition often goes undetected for some time...."

The words of the Señora as prophet came back to me: "I am already a dead woman in the eyes of my family and medical science." There, having been diagnosed with "myopia," a far less serious disease than cancer even to a layman, and they were already treating me as if I didn't exist while I was standing right next to them throwing myself against the wall in a red dress.

"You may have a seat back out in the waiting room," the nurse who had seen me said.

Fifteen minutes later Federico came back out. "We got an appointment for you for this afternoon. The optometrist is a very good friend of Doctor Garcia. But we couldn't get it until three this afternoon. Come on. You will have to let me drive you now."

Was he talking to me, I wondered as I looked over my shoulder.

It would be three hours before my appointment with the eye doctor. Not enough time to drive back and forth to the hacienda with anything but a rush in between. And too much time to spend waiting around town with an all-too-protective Federico.

"I'm going over to the store for a while," I decided quickly.

"Good. Hop in. I'll come with you and we can tell Maria-Elena together."

"Are you crazy, Federico! If you want to tell her, do it on your own time. I, me, by myself am going to walk over— the doctor didn't say I was too blind to walk, did he?—to my store by myself to check on my business. If you need something to do, you can drive home, bring someone down for the other jeep and go home again. I will take a taxi home when I am finished. So your work is all cut out for you for this afternoon. Now leave me alone."

Federico has never liked being spoken to in this tone of voice.

"Why did you do what you did to me the other night if you want so badly to be left alone?" he said.

"Federico, I have more important things on my mind right now."

"Sure, like bras and girdles, right? You always have more important things on your mind than us. Why do you think this lapse took place to begin with?"

We were not quite shouting at each other on the street by the two parked jeeps. I was beginning to wish I did have an appointment with a psychiatrist instead of the eye doctor.

"So it's because of the store, Federico? Don't give me that shit. Maria-Elena has only been working in it for four years. Were you fucking someone else before that because of the store? What's wrong? Did I stop loving you or love you any less when I went into business? Tell me! Didn't you say at the time that it would be good for me to get out of the house. Didn't you tell me I was driving everyone crazy on that stupid 'farm' with my attempted reforms. Didn't you insist that you should loan me the money to get started instead of me borrowing it from the bank? Didn't I repay the money with interest?"

"Yes. But it was my mother's idea to loan you the money."

"Oh really, your mother's idea? Was it her idea that you should fuck Maria-Elena too or did you think of that all by yourself?"

"I didn't think of it. If you didn't have that stupid business I wouldn't have even met her."

"What! So it's my fault then. I forced you into it!"

"No. I don't mean you forced me into it. I am only saying that I didn't think of it. It was only that she was there when my mother was in the hospital and you would send me over to get the books or something. She was always there and she was always so kind and concerned and asked for you always. It was bad enough that my wife was so rich and famous as if your home wasn't enough for you, but then you started sending me as your messenger boy, too."

"I didn't send you over like a messenger boy. I asked you to go when I was at the hospital with your mother."

"Exactly, and how could I refuse?"

"You could have said no if it bothered you so much!"

He was silent.

"And you could have said no to that cheap little slut when she was so 'kind and considerate' to you."

"That cheap little slut, as you put it, happens to like you very much, Rubia. She hangs on your every word. If you tell her that you like her hair short, she trims it every week. If you are wearing a new style, she goes out and gets the new style. She thinks you are very modern and liberated. She tries to be just like you."

"That includes my husband too?"

"No, it wasn't like that, Rubia. It just happened. One day it was raining so hard and it just kept happening and you were indisposed and my mother was dying and she was concerned."

"So she thought she'd help me out by keeping your goddamn cock hard while I was at the hospital with your mother."

"No, it wasn't like that! You make it sound so dirty. I will not give you the details only that it was raining that first time..."

"Federico, I don't want the details. I don't even want to know that it was raining. Can't you understand that I am hurt. That I feel hurt and betrayed. And now you think I should simply forgive and forget because you are under some misguided notion that I was giving you a blow job the other night because you are just too irresistible for me to keep my hands off you."

"Well, you were ready for action that night they gave you the tranquilizer, weren't you?"

"Yes, I was. But it didn't seem proper for you at that time, but it was OK to be fucking your mistress, no?"

"For God's sake, you had thought you had seen my mother dead the night before that—it would have been like taking advantage of a drugged person. You're a part of that—a part of the house and my mother dying. Maria-Elena isn't a part of that. It was only after you came to the den that night that I realized how badly we needed each other and that you were forgiving me even though you were doing it while you thought I was asleep. Don't deny it now, Rubia. What else could you have been doing if my notion was so incorrect?"

Be still, I told myself. It was not the time to tell what I really had been doing. I pulled myself together. I wanted to end our argument at once; I did have more important things to deal with at the moment. I had to think of the Señora only. I answered calmly, no longer shouting, "I was looking—Federico, just looking to see if it was still there."

"To see if it was still there! Do you expect me to believe that? Where else would it be?"

"I don't know—maybe Maria-Elena keeps it with her all the time. Maybe she keeps it in her purse or between her legs when you aren't with her, to comfort you. God forbid you should go a minute or two without a hard-on."

"Well, did you find what you were looking for? Did you see that it can't be screwed off and on so easily?"

Unfortunate choice of words, Federico, I thought.

"Oh, can't it?"

He involuntarily looked down between his legs. I started to walk away. He grabbed my arm. No, grab is not the right word. Grab was the way I had expected him to touch me. But he did not grab. He softly reached for my arm. His hand gently slid down the length of my arm. His gentleness surprised me.

"Rubia," he said with a crack in his voice, no longer shouting. "I'm a man. The opportunity was there and I took it. Maybe I did unscrew it and give it to her. But that doesn't mean I gave her my heart and my soul, too. My heart and soul were with you always. You were exhausted. You were with my mother. I could not come to you then. I'm sorry. I am just a man. Forgive me."

Calmly. Very calmly. "No, Federico. Any argument except 'I'm a man.' Does it make Juan Ortega or Don Juan or any male on the street any more of a man to follow his cock wherever it leads him like a dog on a leash. No, Federico. Not 'I'm just a man.'"

He did not answer. I walked to the store. He surreptitiously followed me from a distance in the jeep. When I entered the store, he was parked across the street up a ways, sitting behind the wheel, looking the other way.

19

≈ ≈ ≈ ≈ ≈ ≈ ≈ ≈ ≈ ≈ ≈

The shop bell tinkled. The thick beige carpet cushioned my step. A well-dressed young woman greeted me. I had never seen her before.

"Good day, Señora. If there is any way I may assist you, I am at your service."

"No! No! No!" said one of the Spinning Marias sitting on the stool behind the glass and chrome counter. She was wearing a dress I'd never seen before—an elegant gray dress with a pink scarf at the neck. She was dressed up. She was not in the back room spinning the ancient lace as she had been for centuries before. And her hair was curled and...I moved a little closer, squinting as if I really were myopic. The hair net was gone! But no, as I moved closer I saw that she had replaced the hair net with the little sparkles with a more subtle, more invisible one. She was ignoring me. She was speaking to the young woman who had asked me if I needed assistance.

"Teresa, no. This is the owner of the store. You must not greet her as if she is a customer in need of assistance."

"I'm sorry, *Tia*," she said blushing, "I did not know."

"Well, this is *Rubia's*, you know. How many blondes with blue eyes are there here?"

"I'm sorry," Teresa said to me. "Such a coincidence."

"No, not a coincidence, this is the Rubia. But it is not important. What if Rubia were just a regular customer? You still must not greet her so quickly. When a customer comes in

144

the store, first you must allow them time to look for a moment, to adjust, then you greet them. But it is not important. You will get it before long. Rubia, this is my grand niece, Teresa."

"Hello, Teresa."

"Hello. Please excuse my mistake."

"Oh, no problem."

"You are not to worry," said the Spinning Maria taking me to the back. "Everything is being taken care of. Business is good for this time of year. The store is only empty now because it is siesta time, of course, but I am keeping the store open at lunch now because there are so many new people to train. But don't worry, the new ones are getting minimal salaries until they are fully competent.

"Maria has taken over the bookkeeping" (meaning the Spinning Maria with the foot problems and the bad back, I sensed). "She is in back finishing the receipts for yesterday. She was tired of making lace, no? And Maria" (meaning the Spinning Maria with the little cigars, I sensed) "is in back teaching Isabella and her daughter and Juanita how to make the lace.... I hope you don't mind that I've kept the lace making in the family. I know that you know how to make the lace and when your daughters are older, I wouldn't mind if they learned, but I wasn't just going to teach any of our Marias the trade secrets—some of them don't even know how to sew! However, there are a few things you must show us with the books. On the foreign orders, do you use the rate of exchange from when they placed the orders or when you receive the orders? But that is not urgently important."

I was stunned. We walked back to the office. It had never looked cleaner or more organized in the back.

"I hope you don't mind, Rubia, but I have had to be a little firmer with the other Marias. Maria-Elena just didn't have your presence and they were slacking off a bit. But Maria-Elena was only *assistant* manager. It is easier for me because

I am older and I am not afraid to be promoted. I am a manager, if you don't mind and if you are pleased with my work, of course. But that is not important now."

Where was Maria-Elena? Did she make the Spinning Maria manager? If you are an assistant manager, can you promote someone else to a position over you?

"Where is Maria-Elena?"

"Well, I don't know. She has not come back since you fired her."

"Since I fired her? I don't understand. I didn't fire her."

"Well, she thinks you fired her. But don't worry, you made the right decision. The other Marias don't know but I knew she was after your husband. She was in tears in the back the day you ran out of here. She said, 'She knows, she knows. Oh, I didn't mean to hurt her.'

"'Tell it to the confessional,' I told her and she ran out. Maria brought over her severance pay last week to her apartment. She didn't deserve it, but business is business. Now, how is your mother-in-law?"

"She is dying. But she has much strength. More strength than anyone could have imagined."

"Ah, God is with her."

Tears started to roll down my face.

"Rubia, you must not cry. You must rest. You look tired. The couch still waits for you at siesta time, Rubia. We used to say, when you were new and not Spanish yet, how well she sleeps for an Anglo at siesta time!"

"But I must go the doctor's at three."

"It is not important. We will wake you with plenty of time."

Just like the elves, I thought. Just like the little cobbler's elves I thought of when I first found them spinning.

The Spinning Maria spread the sheet over the old green couch. I took my dress off. Just like old times. Except that she

did not hum "To Love Somebody" as she left.
I slept.

20

≈ ≈ ≈ ≈ ≈ ≈ ≈ ≈ ≈ ≈ ≈

I took a taxi home with Federico following not too discreetly in one of the jeeps. Behind him, Juan Guernica, friend and police chief, drove the other jeep. Then Juan took the taxi back to Saint.

"Did Maria-Elena upset you?" Federico said as we walked up to the house. "Did she say something to upset you? Is that why you haven't said a word to me since you left the shop?"

(So he didn't know that Maria-Elena hadn't been to the store since that day. Hadn't they spoken, I wondered.)

"I wasn't talking to you before then either."

"Rubia, we spoke at length outside the doctor's office."

"Yes, we did. Well, I didn't mean to."

By the time we sat down to dinner, the universe was buzzing with talk of my alleged myopia.

Ada was crestfallen. She looked as if the Pope had issued an edict stating there was no God.

"What do you mean?" she said. "That it isn't a miracle? Only that the doctor says you are blind?"

I kept winking at her during my story, but apparently she thought this was part of my eye condition.

"*Dios mio*," she said and made the sign of the cross, "but the Señora was always such a holy woman but now it is only your eye disease."

Finally, I got her aside in the kitchen while everyone was moving into the dining room to eat. "Ada," I whispered, "listen to me. If the Señora is a very holy woman and God performs a miracle that not everyone understands, then it doesn't matter what the people who don't understand it call that miracle, does it?"

"What?" she said. But she began to see the light by the time the main course was served and then winked at me several times. In case I had missed her winks, she called me into the kitchen between courses on the pretext of identifying a utensil which she said she was not sure was usable for everyday or something I used to mix the medicine.

"I think I understand," she said. "The doctor, who is a very learned man outside of miracles, which they don't teach in medical school, says you are blind, but the priest who is a man of God says that miracles happen every day. So the priest who has higher authority on such matters is more correct, no?"

"Yes, Ada, that's one way of putting it."

"But why then don't you say so for truth's sake, Rubia?"

"Because some people are like doubting Thomases like Father Tamaso said and need lightning bolts before they believe."

She still looked doubtful.

"Or to put their hands into Christ's wounds..." which was laying it on thick but it seemed to remove Ada's doubt.

"I'll play along, but can't they see that you *are not practically blind?*"

"I don't know, Ada, God works in mysterious ways."

"Well, I'll do my best then."

Maybe I was wrong to lead Ada on that way, but I needed a compatriot and at that point it did not matter to me whether the "vision" of the Señora was caused by the direct hand of God's intervention, a less spectacular medicinal mix, or even by the Señora's stubbornness. It all came down to the miraculous to me.

Rosa was happy that the doctor had confirmed her suspicions that there was no real apparition, but a little put off that such a mistake could have been caused by a correctable vision default and not by insanity.

"So maybe you weren't trying to poison my mother, only that you are blind," said Rosa.

"Sorry, I can see up close and I still wasn't trying to poison your mother."

She clucked her tongue and turned to Federico.

"Are you sure, Federico, that you talked to the doctor personally, by yourself, and he said it was nothing more than myopia, nothing more?" Rosa said to Federico more than once. But all in all, dinner was quite merry with everyone contributing stories to confirm the doctor's diagnosis. Federico retold how he drove behind me on the way to Saint and how I was all over the road (he said). Señor Rodriguez said that he had seen me trip over the dog more than one time lately. All the girls told of repeated poor performances in my Scrabble playing, which they related to an inability to see the letters. Even Juan Ortega said, "Maybe that's her problem—sometimes she looks at you but she's not really looking at you."

The girls were very giggly; it has not been often in the past few weeks, in the past year, that we have sat down to a chatty pleasant dinner. "Tell the story again, *Tia*, tell about Doctor Santa Claus and the cuckoo clocks," one of Rosa's juniors said to me.

"Do not embarrass your aunt with that ridiculous story again," Rosa said. She tries to keep as much joy as possible out of the proper little lives she's made for them.

"It does not embarrass me, Rosa."

"You should not make the children laugh at an adult, Rubia."

I ignored her and told the story to the girls the third time that evening: "I walked up to the address Dr. Garcia had given me and I thought I had made a mistake because it was a jewelry store. So I went in to get directions to the right place and a man who looked like Santa Claus said, 'Señora Rodriguez, you are right on time.'"

"A doctor who looks like Santa Claus who has a jewelry store!" giggled Patricia again.

"'Are you Doctor Fuentes?'" I said.

"'Yes,' he said.

"'But this is a jewelry store, no?'

"'Yes,' he said. 'You have come to the right place. I am an eye doctor, but I always liked making the jewelry for the frames the best, so I gave up the doctoring part and now only make glasses and jewelry.'

"He took the paper from me that Doctor Garcia had told me to give him and I followed him into a back room where every space on the wall was covered with paintings and thousands of cuckoo clocks. Doctor Fuentes put a little machine..."

"Call him Doctor Santa Claus," my youngest niece said.

"Don't make fun of a doctor, child, even if he has fallen. You see, Rubia, what you make the children say."

"All right," I said, "Doctor Santa Claus put a little machine in front of my eyes with lenses in it and kept switching the lenses and told me to tell him which one was the best for me.

"But all the lenses were switched so fast and all the cuckoo clocks and the bright pictures looked like a kaleidoscope and I could not even find the poster on the wall with all the letters on it like they have at Doctor Garcia's.

"Finally I stepped away from the machine and said, 'I am sorry, Doctor, but I can not even see the letters.'

"'What are you talking about?' Doctor Claus said. 'There are no letters. You are supposed to be looking at the pictures of the waterfall on the wall in front of you and tell me when you can see it best! Haven't you ever had glasses before?'

"'No, I'm sorry,' I said and I put my eyes back behind the machine with all the lenses, but just then all the cuckoo clocks in the room came to life...." And the girls joined me with the chorus: "CUCKOO, CUCKOO, CUCKOO!"

I left the story there and did not elaborate any further. I had had a hard time figuring out which lens would confirm my feigned diagnosis but I lost all train of logic after the cuckoo clocks exploded and just took the next one that came along which distorted and enlarged the picture sufficiently. Then I chose a nondescript frame and it must have been all right because all the doctor said was that my glasses would be ready in about ten days.

"A lot of the nuns wear glasses, Mama," Margherita said.

"Yes, I'll be in good company," and promised myself again not to forget to buy her a training bra to get her mind off nuns.

We lingered over coffee after the girls went to do their homework. Señor Rodriguez excused himself to check the horses. I excused myself to mix the medicine. I was out of my chair but not yet out of the room.

"Are you sure, Federico, that you are telling me every-thing *and* that you told the doctor everything?"

"Yes, Rosita," Federico said in a bantering brother-sister voice which I had not heard him use in a long time. "Too bad for you but the doctor said it was only her eyes."

Under her breath but loud enough to be heard, Rosa answered, "And the doctor said that you must sleep in the den because of your wife's eyes, too?"

I do not know if Federico replied. I mixed the medicine and delivered it. I put Margherita and Patricia to bed. I took a nap and waited for the night.

21

"Well, what have you decided? Are you going to stay?" the Señora asked when we had moved through the darkness into the sitting room.

I turned on the lamp and dimmed it. It was darker than the night before when the moon had moved through the haze to make light and shadow. The clouds had been lower and denser all day. It will rain soon.

"Abuela, it has only been twenty-four hours. These are big decisions to make."

"Singular, Rubia."

"Excuse me?"

"Singular—it is only one decision, to go or to stay."

"But it is a big singular decision, no? And I did not have much sleep nor much time during the day to think."

I gave her a synopsis of the day: the doctor, the store without Maria-Elena and the jeweler-eye doctor.

"Now that they think I am blind and not insane, we will be able to show the doctor how well you are doing with the medicine. I have thought maybe he could spend the night and see for himself. We must find a way to get you more medicine without..."

"Without killing me, Rubia? And how are you going to get the doctor to spend the night here to begin with? Look how he reacted when you tried to tell him the truth."

"Well then, the nurses, we could convince the nurses."

"You waste time with your plans for me. I have been over this myself. We are not on the first string of nurses you know. With Rosa's bickering, supervising, and constant rescheduling and with my attempts at proving my strength, pulling out IV's, and my astonishment at finally, so late in life, being able to behave any way I want, we have scared all the good nurses away. There are rules to every game and I didn't know them yet. These are mostly new recruits. The one snoring in there tonight isn't even a nurse, although I don't think Rosa knows. She's the cousin of the aunt of one of the earlier nurses who sometimes dons a white uniform to sit with unruly patients. It's not that this batch of nurses are unkind, Rubia, only that they are untrained. I do not blame the service. I even consciously helped get rid of the good ones. I have more freedom to roam at night with this one who sleeps so well with the aid of one of my sleeping pills than with the ones who turned me every four hours, put cool cloths to my forehead, and kindly registered my every sigh."

"But I will think of a way."

"My stubborn one, you should be thinking of other things at the present time. I have told you already, it is not a cure. Even as I sit here without pain and without grogginess, I can feel this disease everywhere. I am only thankful to God that I have this little bit of sanity left. And do you understand that I like to be free by myself at night like this? If you gave me the medicine earlier, I would have to put up with everyone's disbelief and if I still had time after that, I would have to put up with Rosa's organization and neighbors and who knows— social teas from my bed.

"It is only recently that the medicine has worked this well. And now, who knows how much longer this will last? I don't think I could handle having a social tea during an off day. Even if you are able to be consistent with this new mixture, how can you guarantee that Ada's relative's cure, which you say you have been adding, will be consistent. It might contain lizard eggs or something strange which may change with the lizard's diet.

"Only for my husband I feel badly. It is so hard for him. It hurts him so much to see me die. Sometimes I stand outside his door at night and it is all I can do not to go to him. But it has taken him so long to accept the fact that I am dying. To give him false hope now would be cruel. I would like to hold him once maybe, feeling well, not like an old sick woman clutching to him. Ah, Rubia, I miss him the most."

She grew silent. I leaned forward and held her hands on her lap on the white gown. I left the silence alone.

It hit me then. It hit me differently then. I did not think of death like she did, like the strict Catholics did: that after living a good life and being forgiven for the things that were not so good, you died, went to heaven where you saw God, bright lights, and long-lost friends. I had thought of death and birth as some sort of bigger plan, a universal samba with rest periods in between. My unregimented philosophy allowed me much freedom. It allowed me to be filled with awe and inspiration at religious pageantry one day and to curse vehemently the Church which enslaved the Indians to the duty of poverty the next. And then not to worry about it for the rest of the week. It was all part of it. It was all bigger than me. But I had avoided the nasty little details of death—the empty bed, the empty chair at the dinner table which would be empty forever; details like standing outside your husband's room after fifty years of marriage and wanting to hold him but not wanting to break his heart with false hopes. The new panic crystallized and my heart iced with rapid panic. Petty differences dissolved in the face of empty beds and empty chairs. Even Maria-Elena became a petty difference! You don't have to be old and have cancer to die, I thought. What if I should never see

Federico again? What if he should never wrap those bear paw arms around me when I went to sleep? What if I should never sleep again knowing even in the deepest of sleeps that he was beside me? What if his warm bed smell should drift through the open window through the breeze and the seasons and just finally never smell of him again?

I know it was cruel to say but my panic had taken away any sense of subtlety: "Abuela, if you knew then, when you were the young girl of the story you told me yesterday, if you knew, really knew then, what it might feel like to die and leave forever and ever... to stand outside your husband's door, would you have 'sent' him away? Would you have gone to Mario?"

"Rubia, I did not know then that you cannot have everything the way you want, but even then I knew that there were rules to every game, and love is one of those games. I would not have what I have had for my lifetime if I hadn't played the game. If I had been a good martyred wife, like Rosa, no? and accepted my husband's actions without thought to my pain, then I would have lost without even playing. Maybe if he had been the one never to return, I would have regretted it. Maybe if I had never let him go, then I would have forgotten in time... but it wouldn't have been the same. But why do you ask me questions which have no answers? Is it because of Federico? Do you think that you should forgive him his sins and invite him back into your bed this very night just in case either of you should die by the morning? It would be a nice gesture for you to make and it would make me very happy (provided neither of you did die during the night) and would assure me before I died that you would stay here, except that you would both wake up in the morning and the morning after. And where, after so many mornings, would you go with your desperateness?"

I did not answer. The way she put it before my eyes, the pillow already would not smell so sweet. I shook my head.

"Or maybe you mean that you just leave and just cross off this part of your life so you would not have to stand outside his door some fifty years from now. Ah, Rubia, even if you could forget this part of your life, you would never be able to forgive. You would always wonder why, if he was the one who broke the trust, why it had to be you who had to leave. And you could never get far enough away, Rubia, even if you moved to the North Pole and died, you would never feel far enough away from such a large part of your life. You carry all unfinished business with you wherever you go. Maybe I shouldn't have stopped you. Maybe Juan Ortega shouldn't have come home drunk and singing and maybe Pepe shouldn't have started to bark and maybe I shouldn't have practically fallen into the room. Maybe it shouldn't have happened that way and now you would be standing with a 'limping' husband with tears in your eyes and a grin in your heart. But he is my son and there are other ways. At least I am not like my mother-in-law and just tell you to accept it. You do love him, no?"

"Yes, but there is no war to send him off to."

"No, there isn't. But you will find your own way and a less violent way. You are smart and you know how to use power."

I was drifting away and tired.

"I have thought much about this hacienda lately, Rubia, or maybe I am only realizing decisions I came to long ago. You have already shown that you know how to organize and expand and you are in touch with the times. You have done wonderful things with what started out to be such a small business."

"Oh yes," I said, not following her train of thought too well. "Federico told me today that it was you who insisted on loaning me the money to start. I did not know that, Abuela. I am very grateful."

"It was nothing, Rubia. How else could I see that you had a head for business and could keep books? I already knew you had a spirit for reform and that was and is now more than ever important to me. The land reforms which have started to take place in the rest of the country will come here soon too; we are not as isolated as we once were. I only had to see that you had a good head for business in a practical sense. The men might manage the workers here but I control the bookkeeping and the orders and the money. I couldn't very well have you apprentice with me with my own daughter here. She has a good heart, Rubia, like Federico's mother (she even looks like her), but she is too frivolous and has no head for business. I knew that long before my son brought you here. And look how well you did on your own."

"Abuela, thank you again but much of that was an accident. I don't know anything about a hacienda or buying and selling wood. Federico would know that."

"No, Rubia, I know that. Federico doesn't know the intricacies of the bookkeeping and the money and my husband hasn't done it since I took over at least fifty years ago and a lot has changed since then. But even if they were to learn like you will learn, they are steeped in tradition. When the land reforms come from the government, they would not know how to make concessions and the government would just take the land away. You are a rich woman. You think, why should I bother? You are worth how much in Yankee dollars? I am not talking about measuring wealth in dollars—I am talking of land, of real power, of land for my grandchildren and their children. Of power, Rubia, of making it the 'same' again between your husband and you. Here is your opportunity. You don't *have* to send him off to any war.

"You say you know nothing about the hacienda, but you know far more about it just from being here for so long than you did about bras and girdles and lace and robes when you started your business on a whim—out of boredom, no? And you have set up your business to run without your constant care and that is the sign of an executive. How can you say it was just an accident?"

She was so vibrant and so excited, almost mad for a moment. I hated to disappoint her. "It *was* just an accident. Abuela, I just happened to take over a lace and linen shop which had yards of left-over lace and three stubborn old women who wouldn't stop making more lace. It was not planned. I just didn't know what else to do with the lace. I started designing the gowns because I wanted to get rid of the stuff. It was just a lucky accident and it was the use of that *accidental* lace that made me successful and not the bras and girdles. If the lace hadn't happened, no matter how good a business woman I might be, the bras and girdles just couldn't have pulled in that kind of profit."

"*Everything* is an accident, Rubia, if you put it that way. Or fate or the hand of God, if you will—it's what you do with those accidents that make it important."

I drifted off. She kept talking in a fervor about the hacienda and opportunities. But as much as I had been looking forward to this meeting, I had had a busy day and not much sleep and I wanted to hear bedtime stories of her life, not this. I kept thinking how nice my bed would be and how nice it would be if things were the same between Federico and me and we were in the same bed again. And even if things were never exactly the same again between us at least maybe we could somehow start all over again. I missed his big paw arms and his presence and even his power more than I could ever have believed before. I grew sentimental from weariness.

The Señora talked on. But my thoughts stayed with Federico and our little honeymoon room in Cape Cod and our secret Spanish days in the midst of New York's English when "Rubia" meant a precious jewel to me and not "Blondie."

"...what would you do, Rubia?" I caught the Señora's sharp tone in midstream.

"What?" I asked.

"Please pay attention now. This is only a hypothetical question but the details are important and we must talk about details now. I don't know how much time I have left."

"I am sorry," I said. The "not much time" brought me back to reality. "Say it again, please."

"What would you do if a large corporation or the government, let us say, found oil on a portion of land and wanted to buy it?"

"Sell it to them, but just part of the land and then charge them high prices for transportation through the rest of our land and waterways and then maybe work out a labor agreement with the hacienda?"

"Not bad, but no, that would only be the last resort and only if it was the government and not a corporation. You would make concessions but you would *lease* it to them only at the going rate, of course, and then charge high prices for transportation but hold on to the land as far as possible."

"Oh, I see."

"Now what happens if the government starts to emphasize, as it has in other places, land reforms and wants one of the little villages belonging to the hacienda for the people?"

"Lease it to them?"

"No, Rubia. Sell it and sell it cheaply to the people, but only the individual plots of land where they have their houses and then work out some type of profit-sharing program for the workable land there. Do you understand?"

"Yes, I think so."

"Well, I see that you are tired now but think about all I have said to you. I will not see you to really talk again until Monday night and that will give you time to make your decision. This nurse is off for the weekend and a real nurse will be here, so you must not come."

"But what will you do, Abuela? Will you have to stay in bed all the time then?"

"There are many details I must organize to tell you and I can do that just as well in bed as any other place. If the nurse should nod off for a time, I will put the list on paper. If not I will memorize it and I will have time to pray also. It's you who have much to do in the next few days. Go now, you are falling asleep. I will sit here a little longer."

I kissed her.

"Rubia," she said. "It's not like that."

"Like what?"

"Like what you said before. Dying does not feel like you are going away to leave forever and ever."

Out of weariness maybe, I wanted to go to the den to sleep on the couch next to Federico. But it would not have been right. I prayed, as I sank into my empty bed, that we would all live until morning or until I could think of something that would make it right again. There *are* rules to every game.

22

≈ ≈ ≈ ≈ ≈ ≈ ≈ ≈ ≈ ≈ ≈

I become more Anglo everyday.

It is strange to live in a fair-sized city in the middle of nowhere. It is even stranger to be living so far inland when there is water everywhere. I had always lived in an apartment as a child. The Hudson formed my most western border, but to the east, the great expanse of Atlantic was always there, not always seen, but there, offering space to breathe and freedom.

There is water everywhere here, always seen and felt, but it does not offer that illusion of freedom.

In town, you can hear the river at every turn. The mist brings the river daily into your skin and when the rain comes, it floods your soul. There are parts of the river, a part of our land borders it, where you cannot even see the other side. It could be an ocean there if you didn't know it wasn't, if you didn't know you were in the middle of the continent and that you were still somehow surrounded. The river is not something I think about. It is part of me. My mother once asked me to describe it before she had ever come here to visit. I gave her the details. But even then, it was as if she had asked me to describe my right hand or left foot; I could list the details and the whole but I could not describe what it felt like as part of me, as my own flesh.

I visit New York at least once a year. Every so often the girls will come with me. My mother and father have only visited me here twice in all the time I've been married. My sister has never been here. After her last visit here, my mother said, "Why don't you live in Europe if you want to live somewhere foreign." As if the hacienda could put in for a company transfer. I did not grow up with a sense of land, only with changing apartments.

I did not bother to turn on the fan to fill the emptiness when I left the Señora. I peeled like a banana, turned off the light and was asleep before my eyes closed.

I dreamt of the river. I dreamt that I was a child at Jones Beach carting around an old plastic doll I never let go of named Roxann. My mother would say in real life, "You have so many nice dolls, why don't you play with them instead of that old broken one." In reality, I don't know what became of that old doll, but in the dream I lost the doll in the waves at Jones Beach and practically drowned myself trying to reach it. It was carried off and I stood crying and screaming for it. Then I became that lost doll and the water at Jones Beach became the river. Its every tributary, its every turn became less frightening as I found my plastic body floating and bobbing. It became pleasant when I stopped fighting each turn. Every current buoyed me. Every turn was a slide-upon. The smell of jungle was everywhere. The monkeys chattered and laughed as I passed by. I felt the smooth fish brush my legs and tickle my feet. I saw the trees like cathedral arches over my head. I felt the dappled warmth of the sun when the church ceilings moved back. The water turned and twisted me gently in the rapids. The foam was warm. Again and again I moved through the rapids and the foamy sunlight.

I awoke pleasantly out of breath with the slide-upon feeling still in my stomach. I could still smell the jungle. I could still feel the water. I could still hear the sound of the river. It was daylight. The sheet was thrown back. My legs were apart and Federico's mouth vigorously lapping between them. I could not remember what part of the dream I was in. The sensation of being the floating doll left and I became again the screaming hysterical dream child at Jones Beach.

"You bastard. Who gave you the right...what makes you think you have the right! You wouldn't even politely fuck me in this bed two weeks ago, but now you think you have the right to eat me while I'm sleeping in the same bed!"

"Rubia, please," he said while trying to kiss me. "You were enjoying it. You were moving your hips like a belly dancer. You must have come four or five times. You were laughing and moaning. You see how easy it is. We can be lovers again. I did not scream when you were eating me on the couch. I am your husband. You are my wife."

"Get the fuck out of here," I screamed louder and louder as he put his pants on from the floor and left. There was the usual commotion in the hall. I did not care. I swear to God, I thought as I pounded the pillows, if there are rules to every game then I will fuck everything with a cock and then Federico too before I make any decisions around here.

23

≈ ≈ ≈ ≈ ≈ ≈ ≈ ≈ ≈ ≈ ≈

I bathed and showered and showered and bathed to remove the smell of jungle.

"You want to fuck?" I said to Juan Ortega in English loud enough for Federico to hear as I passed the crowd in the front hall. Federico did not translate for him, thank God. I went down to the stable-converted garage by the rest of the stables and got the jeep myself.

I was calmer driving. I decided that all I had to do was seduce Federico's best friend. But I am or was his best friend I remembered, and cried a little at that until I had to stop crying to see the road. I would have to find somebody. Juan Guernica, police chief, was the only person I could think of who came close to being Federico's best friend. But I quickly decided against it. I'd known him for too long, and his wife and mother, and his children go to school with my children.

The thought of not seducing Juan Ortega or Juan Guernica kept me calm or at least kept my anger at a steady pace. No matter what I said, I was surely not desperate enough to seduce my brother-in-law, only that I wanted Federico to hear my anger. If I was to fuck Juan Ortega, it wouldn't count anyway— Juan is a womanizing dullard and even Federico admits that. Juan Ortega disguises his dullness well with flared nostrils and the seering outfit of the flamenco dancer. And if Rosa did fall at his feet one dark midnight in a tourist night club, as I am told she did when they met, and if woman have been falling at his feet long before and since, it is only because my brother-in-law possesses that callous indifference that women have mistaken for centuries as power. He wears that look of disgusted boredom that women have held as the ultimate challenge. It could only be so, I thought as I remembered Emelia, a third or fourth cousin by marriage who seemed so sane and so nice in every other way. It was many years ago at one of the many "getting to know me" teas that the Señora gave when I first came here. They sent me off to find Emelia. I accepted the task gladly as my conversational ability was sorely lacking and I liked Emelia. I would have walked right by the dark stairway at the back entrance had not Emelia's white gloves given her away. By the time I figured out why those white gloves were flailing the air like Marcel Marceau in spasm midway up the stairs and why her white petticoat seemed to be where her collar should have been, it was too late for me to retreat. Juan Ortega was screwing her against the wall midway up the stairs. I stood there like a zombie. Emelia gasped when she saw me. But a minute later when she walked down past me she was calm and unruffled. She gave me a little smile. Juan walked by me with his usual air of indifference. He paused only for a second and without looking at me, he spat on the wooden floor less than a foot from my velvet-heeled shoes. Federico was the only person I told. He seemed to miss the whole point of the story and I spent an hour calming him out of his threats of seriously injuring Juan Ortega for spitting in his mother's house at the feet of his wife. No, Federico would also miss the point if I had enough anger to fuck Juan Ortega. But who would I fuck, I thought, as the traffic thickened. One step at a time, I calmed myself, as the traffic came to a standstill. First I would go to the store and compose myself, put on some make-up and grab a negligee then, then...but I only had a first step!

Where had all the traffic come from? There were not even

any horns blowing. If it were home, if it were New York, there would be horns blowing. It was the first time I could remember Saint having a "rush hour" (if time could be defined that way on this end of America), and everyone looked so happy about it, so content. They all probably thought it was a sign of modernity coming to Saint. I blew my horn. I sat on the horn. The driver in the car in front of me, an old man, got out of his truck and walked back to my window.

"What's wrong, Señora, is your car not working?"

"Oh, it would work fine if it had a chance."

"Oh, you are not feeling well then and need assistance."

"No, thank you, Señor, I am grateful for your concern." I took my hand off the horn. "I just wondered what the hold-up was."

"You are from out of town then. But you have no accent."

"Yes, I am from out of town."

"You are here for the festival then. You are a tourist."

"What festival, Señor?"

"*El Festival de la Madre Consagrada de la Goma.*"

"Isn't that earlier in the year? Isn't that already over?"

"No," he said. "Perhaps you are thinking of last year's festival."

El Festival de la Madre Consagrada de la Goma (The Sacred Mother of the Rubber—it sounds less blasphemous in Spanish) dates back to Saint's rubber boom beginnings. It was last year's that I was remembering; I had missed it along with the traffic because the Señora was in the hospital. Juan Ortega had led the Spanish dancers in the parade. There had been a fight at home because Rosa did not want him to dance. Juan had told her that there were only two visitors allowed at once in the hospital. And although we rarely had less than four in the Señora's hospital room at one time, Rosa has great respect for rules and Juan danced. He wouldn't be dancing this year unless I had missed the argument. Traffic was backed for miles. It was half an hour before I could turn down a back street to weave a longer, less time-consuming route to the center of town. I ended up parking blocks from the store. By then I was somewhat relieved with visions of suave reporters and horny male tourists who came in small numbers to the festival each year and who would make my task easier. The traffic became meaningful. I was carried along with the crowd. I was driven by a revenge which translated easily into horniness. Every male stranger held potential. I felt a power between my legs which had never been power before. I was conscious of my crotch with every step, with every movement of my legs. The streets grew more crowded. The music grew louder when I reached Rosario Square. The parade was passing before I had a chance to cross the street to the store. The religious procession had already passed. I could see the back of the four-foot *Madre Consagrada* carried upright on a wooden platform by six men. After the altar boys, the professional Indian dancers came. The men wore loose white cotton peasant outfits and sandals. The women wore bright circle skirts and were barefoot. Men with guitars and wooden flutes flanked each side. The dancers twirled in between. Men dressed in animal costumes followed. Some had elaborate wings of fire crackers exploding. A child held high on his father's shoulders in the crowd began to cry with the fireworks and was transferred to the waiting arms of the mother. Next came the "Spanish" dancers. This was the group my brother-in-law usually led but he was not there.

The men in the Spanish dance troupe wore tight black jumpsuits woven over wire-tight muscles and high-heeled shoes. Their flat black hats were held in place by leather strings, although they never moved their heads when they danced, not even an eyeball. The women had twisted piles of dark hair at the back of their necks. Their skirts were flounced in many layers beneath tight bodices and puffed sleeves. All that was missing was the thorny rose in mouth, but each managed a look of professional pain without it.

The real "folk" dancers came next. Small bands of unorganized dance groups from the surrounding scattered villages brought up the rear. I finally crossed the street between them. Down the block, the store was still open. The Marias and the Spinning Marias' new additions were out on the street in front watching the rest of the parade. I greeted them and told them to stay where they were. There were several police cars by the store directing traffic and keeping peace. Juan Guernica in full police chief uniform approached me by the door.

"Hello, Juan, this is quite a crowd. I was just thinking about you." I blushed at my own words as if he had read my mind.

"Why don't we go inside where it is more private," he said. "Where we can be alone."

But I didn't want to seduce him! Was it possible that he knew it had been on my mind a short time ago? He had never approached me like this before. I must have been exuding a strong animal odor. The shop bell tinkled behind us.

"I don't know how to say this, Rubia. Maybe we should go to the back room to talk."

"We can talk privately here," I said. The shop was empty but we could safely be seen by anyone who turned around from the street.

"Well, I just might as well say it. I came here because your husband called and wants you arrested."

"Oh, really? You are here to arrest me and for what may I ask?"

"Don't get me wrong, Rubia. I didn't tell him that I would arrest you. I didn't tell him that I wouldn't arrest you either. I just promised him I'd come and talk with you. He was very upset."

"And what are the charges, Señor Guernica?"

"I didn't say I was going to arrest you."

"Well, on what charges are you perhaps going to arrest me?"

"Driving without your glasses was what Federico wanted me to arrest you for."

"But that is absurd. I just came from the eye doctor's yesterday and it's not even stamped on my license yet. Nor am I driving a car right now. Are you thinking of arresting me for watching a parade or walking down the street without my glasses maybe?"

"Please, Rubia, calm down. Federico was upset. He said that you left there driving too fast and said he was worried after the doctor told you yesterday that you couldn't see to drive."

"So where does the arrest part fit in?"

"Well, he was using some strong language. I don't really think he meant the arrest part as long as I get you safely home. He asked me to bring you back or to see that you got a taxi home."

"Well, arrest me then, because that's what you'll have to do if you want me to go peacefully back home on Federico's command. But you'll have to use your handcuffs and the rest of your squad and I'll have every lawyer I can afford breathing down your legal neck."

"Rubia, we are old friends, but please don't put it that way. I can arrest you for disturbing the peace a lot easier than driving without your glasses if you want to get technical."

"Arrest me for that then if it will give you pleasure."

I held out my hands as if for the handcuffs.

He slammed the front door behind him. The shop bell tinkled.

I spent much of the afternoon roaming the streets with a

new peach negligee rolled up in a ball at the bottom of my purse. My anger carried me along. I made eye contact. I tried out different ways of walking, sometimes striding with my head thrown back and my shoulder bag flung over my shoulder, other times with a short wiggle-twist step. I smiled. I pouted. I batted eyelashes and seductively twirled a strand of hair around a finger. The only men who seemed to notice were the very young and very slimy. I am not an unattractive woman. Maybe I was wearing the wrong clothes. Maybe it would have better served my purpose if I had just put on the peach negligee and walked around in that.

By late afternoon, most of the festivities had moved to the church grounds. There was dancing and music and booths of chance. I grabbed some chicken and rice at a concession. I met one of the younger Marias from the store who told me that she thought it was wonderful that I was at the fair ("you must be going loco cooped up in the house all day long") and asked where Federico was. A man from the hacienda name Jorge introduced me shyly to his wife's family. I spied some nuns not too far off and decided to go. As I left, a young policeman at the gate appeared to be headed for me but I pretended not to see him and slipped through the crowd.

Bars, I thought, sitting at a small round table over a glass of white wine in the lounge of the Hotel Buena Vista, bars are the place to meet men. I met my husband at a bar far shabbier. Only it didn't seem so shabby as I had not been there to meet a man. This bar was classy enough to be called a lounge. A trio played watered-down tangos. Ice and glasses clinked. It was an early supper crowd—businessmen and tourists; most of the natives were still at the festival. The chandeliers were muted. Candles on the small tables melted onto linen table cloths. I awaited my fate like a punishment, although I couldn't put my finger on why I should be the one to be punished. I knew there would be someone there for me. I pictured someone fat and oily from an oil company.

The waiter brought me a second glass of white wine, unordered, compliments of a gentleman at the bar, he said. I panicked. My image of a fat oil man faded into the image of the man in the blue suit with the salt and pepper hair who bought me a drink fifteen years ago in New York on that fateful day. He had followed me all this time waiting to claim payment for a free drink! But it wasn't him.

"Hey! You *must* be American," he said in English.

"This is America, sir," I replied in English.

"Oh shit, yeah. I gotta stop saying that, but you do *comprende* I see and you gotta be from the States."

His name was Sunny with a "u" and he *was* from an oil company. But he was not oily at all and not ugly. He appeared to be in his mid-thirties with sandy blond hair, blue eyes, tall and executively slender.

And my name? "Beatrice," I said hastily, using my almost forgotten confirmation name. But my clever resourcefulness wasn't necessary—he called me "Apple Pie."

"*Mrs*. Apple Pie or *Miss* Apple Pie?"

"*Ms*. Apple Pie."

"Oh," he said. "That usually means you're a 'miss.' A lot of single women use 'Ms,' I've found, like they're ashamed of not being married. Which is silly—like my ex. She uses Ms. now."

He went on to explain that they should have never been married in the first place. Not that they didn't get along—career conflict. He wanted her to settle down and have two kids but she got an offer on a magazine in L.A. and damned if he was going to leave New Jersey. He couldn't blame her. It was in the blood and two writers were one too many writers in a marriage anyway.

"Oh, you're a writer?" I asked politely. It was easy. I just smiled and nodded and asked the right questions. When I got nervous, I would study his polyester suit.

"Yeah," he said, "nice stuff, human interest stuff, 'people' stories. Like this assignment..."

"You're here on assignment?"

"Why pay to see the world? The industry pays my tab. It's like this, Apple Pie—the company *needs* people down here. Their *own* people—like managers and supervisors. Their *own* people travel with their families and they're not going to send small children and wives out into the wilderness so they send me into the wilderness first. I get the lowdown. I tell them how it *really* is. What the natives are *really* like. What they eat. Where they go to church. Where to send the kids to school. The customs. The traditions. Like the festival today—I covered it. So I get the entire 'people' story together and we get it all printed up in a little brochure and BINGO!—instead of vanishing into the wilderness, the wilderness vanishes. They feel right at home even *before* they're transferred. That's the magic of the written word.

"Now you tell me what do you do. No, no. Let me guess. You're not a writer—I don't mean that as a put-down. I mean you just don't look like the ex. You just don't have that look she had. But you're a businesswoman, right?"

I nodded. Was he real? The pale green suit reflected no light, but his eyes sparkled at his own amusement.

"OK, and you're here for the festival, so your business has something to do with the festival. Right, Apple Pie?"

"No, really I'm just here for the holiday."

"Don't let our company brochures fool you, Apple Pie. This really *is* the wilderness. *No one* comes here for a holiday. Unless your business *is* holidays. You'll have to help me here— travel agent? Costumes? Firecrackers? Besides, you look like a lady with a purpose and not on a vacation. If you were on vacation you'd go to someplace like Las Vegas. You just look too American."

My fantasies were no match for his. "No, nothing as exciting as firecrackers," I said. "Clothing: woman's, import and export. And since I was already here, I thought I'd stay over for the festival."

And we chatted. Was I from New York? Yes, he thought so. Why we were practically next-door neighbors.

"How long have you been here?" Sunny asked.

"Too long."

"Ha, ha. Me too. I've been to a lot more exciting places, let me tell you, but look, really, this place is a lot more interesting than meets the eye if you're into historical-type places. More wine?"

"No thanks." I wanted my eyes wide open for the event.

"Hope you don't mind if I have some more."

Was I hungry? He ate steak while I gnawed on a shrimp cocktail. Would I dance? He was not quite as uncoordinated as I had expected. If it had been rock and roll and not a samba, he would have done just fine. He had Spanish in high school, a little rusty, but it's all coming back, no problem. He gave me a brief history of Saint including Indian ruins which do not exist here, conquering conquistadors who never reached this far inland, and cocained Indians who did not chew the mild coca leaf but rather snorted fine white powder at disco parties.

"But don't worry," Sunny said, "the drug part is not going into the brochure. We have enough drug problems at home."

"That's a wise decision."

"All in all, this assignment has been a piece of cake. Except for being homesick. I've been here eight days. Not a long time, but it's just so different. I think that's why I'm already homesick. How 'bout you, Apple Pie? Here we are, two exiles in the wilderness. You homesick, too?"

"Well, yes. I feel very 'American' as you put it."

"You know...it's still real early and I've got something

that'll make you feel a lot less homesick. Might even cure us both for a little while. Are you game?"

"Sure, why not?" I tried to sound casual.

"That's the spirit."

It's so easy, I thought. Except that my hands were cold and my head was reeling and not from passion.

He paid the check and led me by the hand. My heart pounded harder and the ice from my hands worked its way up my arms and down my feet. We passed the elevators. We wound our way through long empty corridors on the first floor. This *could* be the way to his room, I thought. They *do* have rooms on the first floor of hotels in out-of-the-way places. Your children, a saner voice interceded, think of your children. If you want to fuck, then do it in broad daylight out on the street. Don't let them find your body two days later in a remote underground passageway. Dear God, please don't let me die here, for the sake of my children. I promise not to discourage Margherita from becoming a nun. I'll light a candle every day and pray that she does become one. And if Patricia, my baby, wants to become a nun too, I'll even let them cut off her hair for the black habit.

When the carpet stopped and the floor turned into linoleum, the sound of our footsteps sent me into a full alarm.

"Sunny, where are we going?"

"Come on now, Apple Pie. We're almost there. Show a little pioneer spirit."

I saw a sliding glass door. There was a pool outside it in a well-lit courtyard. We were at the other side of the building. My panic eased.

"I should make you close your eyes for this but...DA DA!"

He led me into a room on the right. It was humanly empty but electronically alive. The room bleeped, lit, and twirled. Electronic arcade games filled each wall of the small room.

I smiled. I took a deep breath.

"Shit, I knew this would make you happy. Is this a cure, Apple Pie, or is this a cure? I'm putting this place in my brochure, too. The hotel just put this in for the oil company people they're expecting. You see, this really isn't a wilderness, I just used that to get you here."

The polyester pockets provided endless coins. I had never played these games. All Palisade Park and Playland offered years ago were pinball machines. I lost horribly at Invasion from Mars, Star Scouts, Pac Man, Electronic Bowling, Galactic Wars and Planetary Rovers. "Hot damn," he said and, "geez, holy shit."

He did not seem to mind that I offered such poor competition nor did he gloat. He was totally absorbed. I was so relieved that I got somewhat absorbed too, trying to beat my previous scores as encouraged. I emptied my purse, discreetly so as not to reveal the peach negligee, for more change.

"OK," he said, "I've been holding out on you. I've got enough left for four more games and I'm gonna put them in all at once. They're yours. But you have to really concentrate and listen to my instructions."

He stood behind me and Galactic Wars. "To the left," he said. "Fire, Apple Pie....To the right!...Now get out of there, you've used all your missiles in that location, so move!" He kissed the back of my neck. I got flustered. My neck is my weak spot and his kiss was not as dry as I expected.

"Concentrate on the game now, Apple Pie." He gave little kisses and big kisses up the down of my neck. I tried not to hear as I heard the zipper on the back of my dress. I tried not to watch as his hand slid under the loosened dress and around the front.

"What nice apples you got there, Miss Pie."

I concentrated on the little Galactic space ships turning circles. One ship looked like a cockroach lost in the cosmos.

My spaceship avoided a meteorite by a microsecond. The spaceship with the tiny bird's feet danced around the electronic cockroach and ate it. Was it possible there in the room? My crotch felt heavy and began to throb. He was kissing my left shoulder. My spaceship twirled off into infinity and came back out by an avalanche of space boulders.

"That's good, Apple Pie. A dangerous maneuver, but your points are multiplied by a thousand in this galaxy."

I felt something hard rubbing on my back. Yes, it would be possible here. I wouldn't even have to turn around. Just bend over the galaxies.

"Watch it!" he said.

Just lift up my skirt, I thought. He put his hand under my dress. So this is how they fuck back home. It was nice. Not sleezy. Not slutty. Just like the Fourth of July. . . .

"Watch. Damn!" he said. "You gotta pay attention and we're out of money now."

The fragments of my ship scattered across the vacuum. He pulled my zipper up.

"I got another cure for the blues, Apple Pie. Two *real* Americans lost in the wilderness. We could go to my room, or yours if you'd like. You got stuff in your room?"

"Stuff?" I asked as I turned around.

"You know, birth control, *protectione*?"

"No, I don't have any 'stuff.' "

"I don't either. I mean I figured if I was with anybody down here, they'd be Spanish. But don't worry, I can get some, I'm sure, unless. . .what time of the month is it for you?"

"I don't know," I said. My mood was gone. I am Spanish or at least my children are, and it was none of his goddamn business what time of the month it was. How dare he get so personal.

"Don't worry, I'll take care of it," Sunny said and we started to walk back.

It was *my* time of the month not his. I was concerned with revenge not with not starting a family. Federico never lost a hard-on over a miniature spaceship exploding and probably wouldn't if a real space ship exploded. It would have been a lot easier if Sunny had let me stay in the galaxies rather than getting so personal.

"You wanna wait in my room? I'll give you my key. Or you could give me your key and I'll take care of business while you change into something more comfortable."

"No, thank you."

"Hey," he said as he sat me down in the lobby under an indoor palm tree. "Hey, you look a little pale all of a sudden. But I know what you're thinking, Apple Pie. I know you're thinking why should I spend the night with a stranger that I'll never see again."

I was really thinking why should I spend the night with someone who had lost a hard-on over an exploding space ship.

He bent over and spoke to me as if I were a child. "On one hand you think, why bother, I'll never see this guy again, but on the other hand, hey look, I'm concerned about relationships and this could just be the beginning. New York and New Jersey aren't that far away. I *want* your phone number. I'd *like* to see you back home. Hey," he placed his hand on my chin, "Apple Pie, that's what you're thinking, right?"

Oh, Christ, only a lunatic could have known what I was thinking and I didn't want to fuck this lunatic.

"OK? A deal?" he said.

"A deal," I said.

"Now you wait right here like a good girl."

Something was terribly wrong, but I couldn't put my finger on it.

He went over to the desk and talked with the man there. Was he asking the desk clerk for *"protectione"*? I walked out the front door while he still had his back to me.

So maybe the truth is that Federico probably wouldn't get a hard-on with *any* kind of space ship around. Maybe it *was* his mother's idea to "allow" me to have my own business. But he tried. Until his "lapse" he had always tried. He tried as hard as his male Spanish brain could try. He tried to understand and he never, *never* spoke to me as if I were a child.

"Maria-Elena's," I told the taxi driver.

"Is that a club, Señora?" the driver asked. "You'll have to give me an address, please."

"Oh, of course. I'm sorry." I tried to remember the Spanish words. "It's residential, not a club, over on the west side of Laguna. Not far, about fifteen minutes. I don't know the address, but I can direct you. What time is it, please?"

"Eleven o'clock."

Good. Not too late. But for what? To wring her little neck?

I told the driver to wait after I paid him, but waved him on when I found her name on one of the little mailboxes lined against the hall.

I had no idea why I'd come, but it felt better than sitting under the palm tree at the Hotel Buena Vista.

"Who is it?"

"Look through your peephole. You know who it is."

"Excuse the mess." Except that it wasn't a mess. Except for a pile of boxes in the hallway. Was she planning on moving perhaps? Into my house perhaps?

I immediately saw a distinct advantage. I was groomed and dressed while she was in pajamas. Pajamas! She didn't get those at my store. We sell gowns or loungewear. I expected her to be in bed in a lace gown eating chocolate bon-bons. I came out fighting:

"So this is where you seduced my husband."

"It wasn't quite like that, Rubia."

"OK, so this is where my husband seduced you."

"It wasn't quite like that either."

"OK, so this is where you two mutually consulting adults fucked your brains out. It's nice. It's a nice place you have here, Maria-Elena."

"Thank you. I mean I'm sorry, Rubia. I mean I am really sorry. Are you all right?—you look so calm. I mean the Señora hasn't... or anything and everyone is all right?"

"Oh, just fine. We're all fine. How are you?"

"Fine. I mean, can I get you anything? Coffee or a drink?"

"Yes, a drink will be fine."

"I'm sorry, all I have is rum or Amaretto or I could make piña coladas."

"How marvelous," I said sarcastically. "Yes, do make piña coladas."

I sat at the table in the dining-living room. The blender hummed from the little walk-in kitchen. Everything was quite modern. Plants dangled in macrame holders. Art posters, tastefully framed, decorated the walls. The couch was beige. There were many pillows.

She poured the drinks from the foamy white pitcher.

"Do you mind if I see the bedroom?"

"Of course. Excuse my impoliteness. I'll give you a tour."

But I just wanted to see the bedroom. What was I hoping to find in there? Federico? Federico's smell? The reason why? The bed was unmade—a double mattress on the floor. There was a small TV on a corner stand, a dresser with a mirror and toiletries, a rattan chair with the pillow I brought her from New York on it. A gray cat slept on it.

"What's your cat's name?"

"*El Puma*," she said.

"*Salude*," I said and raised my glass to *El Puma*. We left the room and sat back outside at the table.

"Look, Rubia, if you've come to tell that you know, I

already know that. And if you've come to tell me to get out of your life, I already have. Federico and I have not seen each other since...except when he told me that you knew."

She gave up so easily, not like the Señora's rival. She finished her drink nervously. "Do have another drink. No, that's not why I came, Maria-Elena."

She did have another. "If you've come to hear me apologize. I do. I am most truly sorry. But I guess that doesn't help very much."

"Maria-Elena, you apologize for everything you do all the time anyway. No, I don't think it'll help."

"I'm moving," she said. "My parents don't know anything, I mean, they don't know who or that he's married. My cousin's family lives in the United States, in Miami. My sister's going to help me pack next week—I've already paid this month's rent. I don't know what else to tell you. I didn't mean any harm."

I sipped gently. She was nervous and gulped her drink down again. They tasted like vanilla ice cream and not like a drink. And she meant it; she was truly sorry.

"This is not what I pictured. You should have a long-haired cat, a Persian maybe. You should be in bed, eating chocolate bon-bons, and pining away. Only the piña coladas. Yes, the piña coladas are right."

She poured herself another. "I have suffered, Rubia. Not as much as you, I mean. Even though I'm not pining away. Only it just happened."

"Yes, I know. It was raining and you just decided to shelter him while I was at the hospital. I know all about it. That's a lot of rain though. How long, a year's worth?"

"No, Rubia, only six months or a little longer, I swear it."

Yes, that's what I'd come for—the details. The details that I didn't want to hear from Federico. I wanted to watch her, to take in her looks, to see her as I had never seen her before—

as my husband's lover. I wanted to know how the apartment felt. I wanted to find the source and confront it. Had it been like the video-game room here? Was that what Federico found here—a taste of the homeland during a state of crisis?

I heard the blender again. "Was it very Spanish?" I asked when she sat down again.

"What?"

"Was it very Spanish, you and Federico?"

"I'm sorry. I don't know what you mean. I've lived here all my life. I don't know how else to be."

"Well, for example, did you play video games and talk about your childhood?"

"I didn't know him when he was a child. We didn't play games. We never went anywhere except here."

"Was that part of the agreement?"

"We didn't have any agreements."

"Oh, just pure fucking then? Did he say he loved you?"

"Yes, well not in those words, I think."

"Oh? Well, did you talk? Did you know that I was at the hospital or home with his dying mother while you were so engaged."

"Rubia, I know this. I guess I knew it then. Once we realized what we were doing we said we had to stop but it just kept happening. I'm sorry. I mean, I love Federico, but I love you too. You were always kind to me. I know we weren't close friends but you treated me like I was somebody, like I deserved to be treated nicely. We talked about you mostly and his mother and dying. He almost cried here one time."

"Oh, that must have called for a lot of comforting."

"No, it wasn't like that. Once a week sometimes. Sometimes we didn't even..."

"Would you stop telling me what it wasn't like, damn it. God, I wish you were a slut. If you don't meet my expectations as a traditional mistress, at least you could be a slut so I could pull out your hair and call you vile names. But here we are drinking piña coladas, you in your baby-blue pajamas telling me what it wasn't like. You lent a sympathetic ear, kept his cock hard for six months and when I found out—inadvertently while you were comforting me—you both decide, as you both love me too much, to stop seeing each other and you're a little sad and sorry and move to Miami. I should be grateful and on behalf of my husband and myself offer you gratitude."

"I'm sorry. I just don't know what to tell you, Rubia. I know you don't think I'm suffering enough. What should I do? I've lost him. I never really had him. Should I fight with you, when I like you? I've already lost my job and I did work hard. And it's too messy here and too sad and I'm moving. I'm sorry but it just wasn't as slutty as you would like it."

Her black hair shook with emotion. Her white skin was flushed.

"Damn. I trusted you. I trusted Federico. Give me a clue. Tell me what it *was* like then. Tell me there's a secret I don't know about between your legs. Tell me you cast spells with your left tit!"

"Fine, Rubia. Here's my left tit." She cupped her breast through her pajama top. "Or my hair, Rubia." She pulled at her hair. "If you want to pull my hair, go ahead. I know I deserve it. I know what I did was wrong. If it'd make you feel any better to call me a slut, then go ahead. I don't know what else to tell you."

There was something wrong.

"Is that was you think, Maria-Elena? Do you think I've come to punish you?"

"You told me it was not enough to be sorry."

"Have a good time in Miami, Maria-Elena. I was there once when I was in high school. I remember it was a nice place. And I hear you don't even have to speak English there now with all the Cubans. Good-bye."

24

The earth is tilted. Not too much, but tilted. It spins on its axis. The clouds go with it. But not the moon. The moon spins around the earth. The earth circles the sun and then the moon goes with it. But not the stars. The sun moves in the Milky Way. The stars go with it then.

Light moves so fast that time stands still at that speed which is why it takes so long to reach you. When you stand and look at the stars, you are making connections with things that happened billions of years before you.

It was dark and it was late. It was not the planet I remembered living on before ringing Maria-Elena's doorbell. The wind had quickened and turned. The clouds moved so fast that I had to stop and remind myself that they were moving with the earth. What took fifteen minutes in the taxi over took forever to walk back. But my feet were moving very fast and my heart was moving very fast and the clouds were moving very fast. Yet time stood still at that speed at that vacuum of night with the stars and moon moving in and out of rapid clouds. Footsteps were very loud. I stood in dark doorways when another person passed. Time stood still then because my heart beat so fast.

The earth is tilted. When I finally got to the jeep that I had parked across town many light years before, gravity and four-wheel drive took over.

But there was still something wrong. Even within the safety of the jeep, things were too bright for so late at night. The sky was pulling away from gravity. The heat which had pervaded, which had saturated the days and nights with various shades of overcast, had risen and was spinning further and further away. The night was clear and electric. Lightning flashed without sound from the distance.

It happened quickly. The wind stood still for an instant, the heavens opened and rain came. By the time I passed the gate, the engine was sputtering. By the time I reached the stables, I could not see past the windshield where phantom hands turned into José who opened the car door. Torrents of wind and water stung my face. The earth swallowed my shoes and groped for the rest of me. I clung blindly to José's arm.

I was shivering when he closed the stable door. My body pounded with exhaustion and cold and delayed fright. Every part of me dripped. I shook uncontrollably. My body hurt from shaking. There was a little room in the back past the stables and restless horses. It had a cot and blankets and in another little room there was a stove and a table. He motioned this way and that. I couldn't understand him. The thunder roared and the rain pelted the roof. What was I doing last year when the first and always the most violent of the rains came—at home playing Scabble with the girls? Sleeping? At the Señora's hospital bedside reading a novel? And the year before that and the year before that? Never had I been outside or out driving in the first downpour. We wrung out my hair with towels. He covered me with blankets. I took off my soaking clothes beneath them and put on an oversized white shirt that he gave me. And I still shook.

"José, I can't understand you. I can't hear you," I shouted repeatedly. He shook his hand in front of his face as if it wasn't important. I pointed up to the thunder and the rain-pelted roof.

"I can't hear you. I can't..."

Then I remembered that he couldn't talk. He couldn't even hear the fury outside which shook me so.

...and everything became quiet for me then.

It would not be fair to say that I had my revenge. There was nothing of revenge. It would not be fair to say that we made love. You cannot make or unmake love. It was more like the earth made us at the center of its circle. Where it doesn't tilt. Where it is very quiet and very still.

25

I know how time is customarily divided. I have a watch. I bought it in New York as a present to myself when my lace gowns were first shown in the Designer's Review. It is unique. Beneath its discreetly hinged cover, it has no hands and no electronic digits. The hidden face of the watch has twelve tiny diamond dots which are stationary while a circle of tiny diamonds and one tiny sapphire move around it. It is very small—not something people comment on. It looks like a gold bracelet with a circle on the inside of my wrist. Its beauty is its simplicity. The only difficulty is presented when its cover is opened and it is used to tell time. I do not open the cover often. And even though I did not open the cover then either, there must have been time that day. It must have been divided like any other day. Beneath the gold cover, there must have been half hours when the sapphire was directly between two diamonds and there must had been many hours when it met the diamond directly.

When I awoke, I asked José, who cannot hear, what time it was. He was sleeping in the chair beside the cot.

"What time is it? What time is it?" I asked. I shook him. I pointed to my hinged watch-bracelet. "What time is it!" I pointed to the wooden ceiling. "WHERE IS THE SUN! WHAT POSITION? WHAT TIME?" I had wakened remembering what had been wrong all day. What had been wrong all night. What that nagging little feeling that everything was not right had really been—I had forgotten to mix the medicine for the Señora. I knew even then that it was not a cure, could not prevent the Señora from dying. But it was not a magic to be overlooked. Was I screaming loud enough? I couldn't hear the thunder. I couldn't hear the rain beating on the roof. "What time is it!"

José pointed to my clothes and held my arm and held me back. I broke his grasp and went through the door to the stable. The quiet was shocking. Was I to bring his silent world with me wherever I went? Would I be screaming forever in silence? I screamed when I saw Federico with one of my muddy shoes in one hand and a knife poised in the other.

Federico spoke and I heard him. "I heard you screaming. Are you hurt? I found one of your shoes in the mud by the jeep. I have looked everywhere for you. I even have the police out. And the storm. Then I found the shoe and heard you screaming."

I know how it must have looked. I was standing there in José's shirt mostly unbuttoned with my left tit exposed and José was coming through the door behind me with my dress over his arm. But did Federico have time to assess all this? Did he realize I was screaming for the time and not for help? Did we stand there in eternity and gaze at each other or did José just come through the door when Federico slashed the knife across his throat? José put his hand with my dress up to his throat and fell backwards. Federico and I ran to him at the same time. I pushed Federico aside. "You're all right," I kept telling José. His eyes were glazed with fright. And the dress I kept pressing to his neck to stop the bleeding must have had its own color before it became José's blood. When I finally looked beneath the cloth it was not spurting like I thought it would be when an artery is cut. Noise like choking and inside coughing began to come from José's throat. It was then that I looked up where Federico was still standing: "Get help, Federico, you must get help." And Federico ran out. Then Doctor Garcia was there with Federico and Doctor Garcia took over and then many people and then the police. I stood in the back with my arms folded over José's night shirt and shook again. They put José in the back of one of the farm trucks with Doctor Garcia. I thought he was dead then, but I wasn't sure. Someone gave me a coat and they helped me back up to the house. It wasn't raining outside. It was morning and it was light, but the heat was gone.

I went up to the Señora's room because that's what they told me to do when I came in. They put a chair for me by the bed. Señor Rodriguez was sitting on the other side.

The Señora held my hand. I don't know how long I sat there. "I would go when... into the light... remember, Rubia?" she said to me, her mouth searching for more air, and then fell asleep for a long time until I knew by her hand that she was not sleeping anymore, only dead.

26

≈ ≈ ≈ ≈ ≈ ≈ ≈ ≈ ≈ ≈ ≈

Margherita and Patricia were in my bedroom. We were saying the rosary. Their voices were like angels from another world. Every few decades, we would cry and I would hold them. One decade, Margherita would dedicate to the soul of Abuela and then the next for José who was in surgery the last we heard. Ada was down at the hospital with her cousin probably saying the same prayers. Federico was down in Saint too, his father had told me earlier. He didn't mention whether he was at the hospital or in jail.

The girls had said that Papa thought José was a burglar. All their questions were too simple for such a complicated world, but I answered them as simply as they were asked. Everything real was too complicated except their little voices and the hypnotic decades of the rosary.

Rosa came to the door and asked to speak with me alone. We stood in the hall.

"No news of José," she said. "They have come for my mother. I gave them the white dress that she liked so much. But now they want underwear so I had to come to ask you, because the underwear is all from the store and all the lace seems too frilly for the Church—maybe she should go without, but that doesn't seem right either."

I kept thinking while she spoke that she should put back on one of her flowered dresses since she had already been

190

wearing the black dress for two weeks before her mother died.

"Give them the lace, Rosa."

"But..."

"If the priests can wear silk while they say the Mass, surely God won't hold a little lace against the Señora."

"Yes. And you don't have to sit with my mother this evening. It is all taken care of."

"What?"

"With the candles and her body, Rubia."

"Oh."

"My father and I are to sit tonight."

"Well, I will take your girls then."

"That will not be necessary. They are with their father."

Patricia and Margherita fell asleep in my bed. It was dark and it started raining again, not with the violence of the previous night's storm, but with the heavy rain of the season. I sat at the window overlooking the courtyard still dressed in someone's unidentified cloth raincoat. I had been wearing José's shirt all day: blood splattered, like some remembered picture of Jackie Kennedy, but hidden beneath the coat. It was silly. Like the hidden face of my watch which so discreetly connected me with real time. It took awhile for me to take the shirt off and get into the bath, as if taking it off would loosen one of José's connections with this earth. As if to bathe away his semen from between my legs would send him hurling unremembered into a dark orbit.

Federico was there when I emerged in his terry robe from the bathroom. I stared at him for a long time. He was sitting on the side of the bed hunched over. He ran his hand through his black curly hair. It seemed strange that he did not look like the stranger he had become in the past month. How was it that his dark hand through his hair was more familiar to me than my own hand, than the touch of my own hair.

"Where are the girls?" I said.

"I carried them into their room. I left the door open and put them in the same bed. They know? About my mother?"

"Yes. We said the rosary for her... and for José also—how is he?"

"He's out of surgery now, but still in the recovery room. The doctors said that he would recover. I left Ada down at the hospital with her cousin. She would not leave until she had seen him she said. It missed his artery by half an inch and caught most of his chin."

"Why? Why did you do it?"

He ran his hand back through his hair.

He spoke slowly. He did not measure his words but he was very tired.

"I knew you would ask me that."

"Would you prefer that I didn't?"

"No, it's just that I knew you would ask me that. No one, not one person asked me. I kept waiting for someone to, but no one did. But I knew you would. I thought of a thousand answers for you while I sat at the hospital and Ada prayed. Even after my father came and told me about my mother, I kept thinking of answers for you. Everyone assumes I thought he was a burglar and that I was a little bit deranged because my mother was dying. I have been over it and over it in my head. I don't know, Rubia. I don't remember. I don't know if I really thought he had hurt you. That was in my mind, with your shoes outside in the mud—or if I did it because I thought you had spent the night together willingly. The storm. My mother so bad and asking for you and looking for you all night and Juan Guernica was reluctant to have the police look for you because I had been so stupid telling him to arrest you earlier and he said that if one of his men saw you they would tell you about my mother dying and asking for you. I was frantic, I know that, but I don't know whether I did it because I wanted to protect you or protect my pride. But it doesn't matter to me anymore why. I did it.

"The second I reached out with that knife, I regretted it. You don't need to be protected or revenged even—not at that cost. Jesus Christ. I almost killed him. I missed by less than half an inch. You're not worth it and I'm not worth it. He's just a boy. He was born here. He can't even talk. He never hurt anybody."

He rubbed his eyes with his hand.

"But he's alive, thank God, and he's all right, thank God."

"Are they going to arrest you, Federico? Are they going to ask us what really happened?"

"Can't you understand, Rubia?—I asked to be arrested. Whatever you did is your business and you tell them what you like. I never spoke for you. They said you took off your dress to stop the bleeding. They said I thought he was a burglar and they won't arrest me for that."

"And if it was not that way? If my dress was already off?"

"Your dress was already off, Rubia, and they won't arrest me for that either—husband defending wife or defending pride— they would applaud me for that. They would parade me as a hero. Oh, God. And Ada's down at the hospital all day telling me to go. 'I understand this was an accident,' she said. 'And I am grateful for your concern, but you should go to your mother now.' And that I would never understand a mother's love for her son. And then my father came and told me. And when I got here, they had already taken her, and my sister tells me to go rest and that you and she had taken care of the underwear and that I'll be on sitting duty tomorrow at the funeral parlor. As if my mother was still alive and had just switched rooms."

And I wanted to confess. I wanted to tell him that she had died because I had forgotten to mix the medicine. That mine was a greater sin simply by neglect. I had been too angry to remember. And if I heard a thousand times more that the medicine was not a cure, I would still blame myself. I wanted to tell him how his mother and I had spoken together and been together nights ago. I also wanted to confess my more venial sins: of spending the day with the peach negligee in my pocketbook (the pocketbook had been returned by someone earlier; they had found it in the jeep; the negligee was still in a ball at the bottom), of avoiding the policeman at the fair, of wanting to call Maria-Elena a slut, of having that nagging little feeling that something was wrong all day and all night, but never taking the time to figure out what it was. Federico could give me the absolution I needed. But it was too much to ask. His every gesture was too familiar. I remember thinking, this is how I thought he would look when his mother died. This is how the night would be. This is how the rain would sound and the dark would be.

"Where is your father? Have you seen him since you got back?"

"Just for a minute. He left for the church with Rosa and then they were going to sit with my mother. Why did my mother want to see you? What did she say to you before she died. My father said that she spoke to you. You don't have to tell me. I am glad she saw you before she died. She was asking for you all night when she was not sleeping and when she could breathe."

"She told me a long time ago that when she died she wanted to die in the daytime when the sun was out. She reminded me of it right before she died. And when she died, Federico, the rain had stopped and it was light out like she wanted. She fell asleep then. She was very peaceful at the end."

"She wasn't gasping or anything?"

"No, she was very peaceful."

27

Funerals are a good example of a greater insanity established to take you away from a present insanity. I seemed the most expendable from the funeral parlor for the continual sittings and rosaries. ("You can be done without as for praying to God," Rosa said to me.) I was only needed in town for the one or two hours at night during the formal wake. The rest of the time I spent making phone calls; receiving food, fruit and visitors at the house; picking up or arranging for someone else to pick up relatives whose faces I barely remembered at the airport; organizing meals and bed space and keeping the dog from tripping old people.

Federico never left his father's side. Except at nighttime when we would crawl exhausted into bed with strength only to give each other a brief synopsis of the day from our different fronts. At least my father-in-law had already been sleeping in a different room by himself for the past year so he did not have to contend with the sudden shock of sleeping alone.

The rain continued. Everything outdoors was wet and muddy. Everything indoors was damp and musty. Sounds were sharp with wet reverberance. The funeral was set for the fourth day because of the influx of relatives.

Dr. Garcia offered a variety of sleeping pills and tranquilizers which were refused by all except an arthritic cousin and Rosa, who developed a strange tranquilizer-induced smile.

She called Ada's second cousin Louisa (who was taking Ada's place while Ada was at the hospital) by the name Teresa and called Louisa's daughter Isabella, Louisa. Whenever I would correct her she would tuck her hair back and excuse herself for interfering. Whenever they would correct her, she would say: "Speak to Rubia; I have all I can do with so much praying."

Margherita kept a three-day running battle with me to be allowed to wear black at least on the day of the funeral. The nuns wore black, she told me; Rosa was letting her daughters wear black and everyone was wearing black except for the "little" children. She had substituted her comb for rosary beads and at most given times when she wasn't arguing with me, she could be found fervently praying. Patricia helped me with the dog and sang little songs to herself.

My mother said she would come to help, but I told her not to. She asked if I would buy some flowers and a mass card here from her. Patricia came with me to the florist in town. I had every available rose in the shop made into a massive bouquet. Patricia wrote out the card from my family. I recited each letter as she painstakingly formed them into her large block print.

There was a small bouquet of tea roses in the window as we went to leave. I am not usually maudlin but I had them sent too.

"Leave the card blank, please," I told the woman. "Just send them as is."

I did not want anyone saying "Ah, how precious" if they read a card saying "From your dog, Pepe."

Father Tomaso was at the rectory. He quietly offered his condolences. I froze in the middle of choosing the mass card. It suddenly became more than I could handle to choose between a simple and elegant card which only bought a hundred masses or a massive gaudy creation which offered perpetual membership in every mass ever said by the entire order of

Franciscans.

"Who is the card to be from? Maybe that will help you to decide," Father Tomaso said.

"From my mother and father and sister," I said. But that didn't help me.

"Why don't you let your daughter decide. Children have a special place with God."

Patricia chose an entirely different card showing "The Little Flower" with eyes fixed and dilated towards heaven under an avalanche of rose petals, which, at a lower price only offered one unannounced mass on a weekday at our own church.

"For the roses, Mama. I like this one for Abuela for the roses."

"I will say this mass personally for your Abuela," Father Tomaso said.

On the night before the funeral, Rosa told me at the wake that I could arrange to have Ada picked up since José was doing very well and Ada wanted to come home for the funeral. I had had fruit and flowers delivered to José's room and had been arranging transportation for Ada's cousins to and from the hospital, but I had not found the guts nor the heart to visit there personally. I drove myself over after the wake while I was still in town. At that hour of night, the hospital was more wakelike than the wake I had just left. It was after visiting hours but I was granted permission to visit the room after much whispering. I would actually have fainted, I think, at the sight of José's bandages covering most of his head had not Ada said, "It is not as bad as it looks, Rubia. I watch them change the dressings. The bandages on the top are only to hold the bandages on the bottom of his chin in place." José's eyes greeted me warmly and his grasp was firm when I took his hand and gave my regards before we left.

There was some small talk in the car, but mostly silence. I grew comfortable with the silence.

"Rubia, there do not have to be secrets between us," Ada finally said. "I know it wasn't an accident, not all of it."

I did not answer. I concentrated on breathing and keeping the car on the road.

"I know the truth that happened that night. Well, at least the important part. But if you prefer that I do not speak, I won't."

"No, Ada, speak. You have every right."

"I have prayed for guidance. I am only mentioning it because my son is getting better now and I will have to know before I take him out of the hospital that he is in no danger from Federico. I pray you haven't told him what really happened. I tried to get to you earlier to tell you not to confess anything except to the priest, of course, but under the circumstances I could not reach you. You have not told him, have you?"

"What exactly do you mean, Ada?"

"Rubia, when you have a child who cannot hear or speak, you learn to understand many things that are not spoken. No one has said anything. I just know. It has changed my son in many ways. You are not a low woman, so maybe it was my son's fault for being a man, but God has punished him."

"Punished him? Ada, he didn't rape me!"

"No. But he shouldn't have picked you. We will go to my cousin's. He will have nothing to do with the house anymore and we will live at my cousin's. He could work in the village. Your secret is safe with me and he has no way of ever telling, of course. But I must be sure you haven't told Federico."

"No, Ada, but if you figured it out by yourself and you weren't even there, why don't you think Federico figured it out? Why do you think Federico did what he did?"

"Rubia, he sat with me for ten hours that day at the hospital. He does not know! He talked only about how could he have done such a thing to poor José, how could he have

been such a fool to have hurt my son. Your husband is a man,
no? If he had really known he wouldn't have regretted hurting
my son. He would have done more than just hurt him, no?"

"Ada, you are talking about your son's life! What do you
think happened that morning?"

"I heard everyone. You were not found in bed or anything. Your husband thought my son was an intruder. I will
make my son promise that it will never happen again. I will
find him a nice girl from the village now that I know. God is
good, mysterious, but good."

"What do you think happened that night that has made
God so suddenly good?"

"You are a woman, no? But you already knew that. And
my son is a man now, no? He even has a scar to prove it."

The girls wore matching blue dresses to the funeral. The
church was very crowded. There was a high mass with words
of dust and resurrection.

The Indians have a saying that the best way to describe
hunger is by describing bread. It must be so. I could list the
number of mourners, the pageantry, and the sad tolling of the
bells. I could recount the stories told of her by friends and
relatives, the eulogy by the priest, the names of each person
who passed in line to offer condolences. I could count the
number of masses which were to be offered in her name, the
flowers in so many bouquets. I could tell how surprising it was
to me to see and feel all the things that were so much bigger
at her death than the tiny closed world centered on the Señora's
sick room that our universe had condensed to before she died.
I could tell how everyone from the most eloquently speaking
priest to the most inarticulate farm worker commented on the
beautiful day—how the story spread how she had wanted to
die in the light and at the moment she died, after such a storm,
the sun had shone and how now, miraculously everyone said,
it was a sunny day for her funeral, right at the beginning of

the rainy season. It is a sign from God, they said. But the best description of the Señora's funeral must be my father-in-law's eyes, which were lost and empty.

PART II
The Recording
of the Miracles

28

The out-of-town relatives and friends gradually left. The girls eventually went back to school.

Maybe it was because the Spinning Marias had things so well under control at the store and I wasn't needed there. Maybe it was because Federico never left his father's side and with José in the hospital, they seemed to have so much to do with the horses. Maybe it was because Rosa had spent so much time "sitting" at the funeral parlor, which she then replaced with "sitting" at church. She had also replaced the tranquilizers with God, but it was hard to tell the difference in her little smile. Maybe it was because Ada, who had taken care of so many things for so many years, was still at the hospital most of the time. Or maybe because the Señora had wanted it that way that the business of the hacienda was left to me. The lawyers brought me papers. The accountants brought me books. Work orders, schedules, bills were all referred to me.

For personal reasons, I was trying to stay as far away as possible from José's affairs. (Ada had already lined up several of the village maidens as potential daughters-in-law.) José was brought back to surgery apparently for some minor plastic reconstruction work. Ada, however, insisted there was more to it than the doctor was letting her know and insisted that I go and speak with the doctor.

I consented even though I did not think there was anything wrong with José that this Doctor Suarez wouldn't tell Ada. But the more I thought about it—why *were* they keeping him in the hospital for so long? If he was doing as well as he appeared and as well as all the reports indicated and if the second surgery was only minor plastic work, why didn't they let him go home or why at least didn't they let him go home between the surgeries? Or was it because they were afraid to let him come back here? Did they know the *real* truth, however that could be construed?

By the time dinner was long over and everyone sound asleep, I had the whole thing figured out: If they weren't going to arrest Federico on attempted manslaughter, then they were going to arrest me for seduction of a minor. Was José seventeen or eighteen? Ada had had him late, in her forties, I think. Her husband had died before José was born. I did not know José's age and could not calculate it with less than a three-year variance. But could a woman be arrested for seducing a just underage male in this country or anywhere? But it wasn't like that, I told my invisible jury, and it was another lifetime ago of extenuating circumstances. Why didn't this Doctor Suarez have us meet him at the police station and save the trouble? Or would Juan Guernica be there when I went for the appointment? Dear Señora, I prayed, please don't let them take me away and don't let anything be wrong with José.

Federico was almost asleep when I woke him. I was going to tell him *not* to tell me that it was not enough time yet since his mother had died. I was going to tell him not to tell me how many things we still had to work out between us. I was going to tell him just to make love to me. But I didn't have to say a word. It wasn't that I wanted love or sex: I wanted to anchor him, I wanted to anchor myself to this place, to this room, again and again, forever and ever.

I was exhuasted in the morning. I was so tired that I was almost calm. My glasses arrived after breakfast, which threw me for a moment. What are these? I thought. Why would a boy come to my door with this package saying that I had forgotten to pick these glasses up at the doctor's? I stuffed them in my purse and Pepe and I left. Pepe went everywhere with me now. If we went in the car, he would curl up into a yellow dog ball and sleep. When I would leave the car, he would raise his head and go back to sleep. When I would return, he would raise his head and go back to sleep.

The office of Doctor Suarez was next door to the hospital in the new professional building. I had to wait over thirty minutes before I saw him. As soon as the receptionist called my name through the small round opening in the frosted glass, I knew what the glasses in my purse were for. The glasses were thick and heavy. I had chosen massive steel grey frames. No one would accuse a blind woman wearing these of seducing a sixteen- or seventeen- or eighteen-year-old. No one would think that the husband of a woman wearing glasses like these would suspect her of anything else but blindness.

"Señora Rodriguez?"

"Yes."

"Please have a seat."

I did not gauge the distance between the desk and the chair correctly. I avoided injury but had to grope a bit. Doctor Suarez appeared young with a baby face under a balding head and a large mustache. He wore a white lab coat over a shirt and tie. He sat at the big desk with his credentials framed behind him. I squinted and unsquinted. He did not appear closer or more distant with my glasses, only distorted, as if I were looking at him with someone else's eyes.

"I wish to speak to you, Señora Rodriguez, because I need your help and because I wish to avoid giving false hope to Señora Ventura and also to avoid any hysteria. Ah, but you, better than I, know how she is."

"Who?"

"Señora Ventura. José Ventura's mother. Your employee, no?"

"Yes, of course."

"Besides, she keeps telling me that you are in charge. I tried to approach Señora Ortega, your sister-in-law, but she told me also that you were in charge. And I understand that you have just had a death in the family, so I did not want to push it. Your mother-in-law, correct? I offer my condolences."

"Thank you. Is there something wrong with José, Doctor? Ada, Señora Ventura, was under the impression that you are holding something back from her."

"Well, not exactly, Senora. Let me get right to the point. Have you ever heard of the expression 'tongue-tied'?"

"Excuse me? I think it means that you cannot find the appropriate words."

"Yes. Yes. But what I mean is the expression 'tongue-tied' as a lay term and a very appropriate one for a birth defect— a congenital shortening of the frenum of the tongue."

I squinted again.

"The frenum is that little piece under your tongue which connects it to the floor of your mouth."

"Yes?"

"I cannot believe it went undetected for so long, Señora Rodriguez. Wasn't the boy ever examined by a doctor? I didn't know that he couldn't speak when I did the emergency surgery on him that first night. It was a delicate area but not a deep wound and I did almost all of the repair work from the outside. It was only afterwards when I got some history from your husband, I think it was, and the boy's mother. But I am so sure. That is why I brought him back to surgery, of course. Señora Ventura is not easy to talk with. 'Just tell me he's going to be all right,' she tells me, and doesn't want to hear any more. And the medical history she has given me is very scanty to say the least. I would have insisted on speaking with you sooner except that I was told about the crisis with the death of your mother-in-law."

He was pacing in front of the desk by then. I waited. Perhaps the glasses were distorting the doctor's words, too. Maybe I was hearing through someone else's ears also. Doctor Suarez looked at me and waited also.

"Doctor Suarez, I am not sure I understand what you are telling me."

"Señora Rodriguez, I am ninety-nine percent sure that José Ventura is not a deaf-mute. That his inability to speak is caused by a congenital shortening of the frenum of the tongue—a defect that is easily corrected with minor surgery, which is why I brought him back to surgery again."

"Doctor. I cannot... I don't know.... But he made sounds. Not words, but sounds, and what about his hearing?"

"Of course he could make sounds. His vocal chords were always intact. He just had very little movement of his tongue. And he is not deaf. I have already had his hearing checked. It was not an easy job even with the fine equipment. Needless to say, he has had much sensory deprivation and to say 'learning disability' is putting it mildly. I am at least sure he can hear *some* sounds and he should be able to speak after this recent surgery. God, such a simple procedure, you just cut through the tissue prohibiting the movement!"

"This is the most incredible thing I have ever heard, Doctor. I can hardly believe it. Not because I don't believe you but only because it is too incredible to believe."

"Yes it is incredible. But that's not the point now. The boy is a minor. It was very, very difficult to get Señora Ventura's permission for the second surgery. And maybe the boy will *never* speak so I did not tell her the whole truth. Now I need your assistance as there will be much therapy involved and I need Señora Ventura's permission to keep José here and to work with him later on an out-patient basis. I will pursue it without your assistance, of course, but it would perhaps be easier with your help."

"Doctor, I did not mean that I would not give you my assistance, only that it was incredible." I forced myself not to blush. The glasses hid half my face anyway. "Doctor, I am very fond of the boy. I will work with you in any way I can. I used to think he was listening sometimes. I used to think, well I still do think he has a sixth sense about him, a sensitivity that transcended his deaf-muteness whether he is a deaf-mute or not. He always brought the cars around to the house even before you asked him to. He took care of the stables which perhaps takes more organization and work than I credited him for."

"Good. Perhaps that was because he could hear. Now, how do you think I should approach the mother? Or would you care to approach her with me?"

"I think, Doctor," as I brainstormed behind the glasses, "that you should *not* tell her. I think we should be there, you and I, but I think that we should tell a priest and after we have explained the situation to him that the priest should tell her. And I know a priest, Doctor, one that Ada likes and respects and who will keep it low key without offering any false hope."

"Well, all right. But I do not want to keep it too low key. I don't want her to think it's not important."

"The presence of a priest will give it importance, Doctor Suarez. José might as well have 'God's will' working on his side, no?"

"I see your point, Señora. It is agreed. Then perhaps we can start to get José used to the idea also. I too think he possesses the sensitivity you say he does."

My head hurt from so much thinking. I shook the doctor's hand, took off my glasses and left.

Father Tomaso was given permission to accompany me the next morning. It was drizzling. Ada was already down at the hospital in José's room and had been for hours. I seated Father Tomaso in the lobby. It took over a half hour to get Doctor Suarez, who could only spare fifteen minutes.

Father Tomaso, Doctor Suarez, and I descended upon the room quickly. Ada was watching the TV. José was sleeping. I was not prepared for Ada's reaction. The blood drained from her face as soon as she saw us.

"I knew they were keeping something from me! And now you have brought the priest!"

We quickly removed her from the room to the visitors' waiting room. It took the next ten minutes to calm her down. Doctor Suarez glanced at his watch frequently.

"Well, if he is not dying, then why are you all here?" Ada said suddenly.

"You tell her," Doctor Suarez said under his frowning mustache.

I did not have much time by the doctor's fidgeting.

"Well, Ada, everything *is* all right. But the hospital needs your further permission to work with José because Doctor Suarez thinks there might be a good chance that José is not deaf and mute."

"What?"

"Well, that José can hear and that he was born with a defect of his tongue which the doctor has corrected with the last surgery and that now José will be able to speak."

"Will be able *to learn* how to speak," Doctor Suarez corrected me.

"And that is why you are here, Father?" Ada said.

"To urge you to give your son the opportunity to learn, Señora."

"Oh, that is why—because you are priest and it is a miracle!"

"Only that we allow God the opportunity to work his many

miracles, if that is his will," Father said.

Ada made the sign of the cross and stood. She looked towards heaven and spread her arms. I had seen that posture before. I had seen those eyes fixed and dilated before in the mass card depicting Saint Teresa that Patricia had chosen for the Señora.

"It is a miracle!" Ada screamed. "It is a miracle from the Señora!"

The day José issued his first words, Ada and I were in the speech therapy lab along with Doctor Garcia and an effervescent speech therapist named Sister Angelina. I had envisioned poetry.

I had envisioned poetry and dark secrets (my own) the day José would speak.

"Ma-Ma." José said. "Mama."

"Mama," José said to Ada.

"Mama, Mama," José called to the crying Ada.

"Mama," José said to Sister Angelina.

"Mama," José said to Doctor Suarez.

"Mama," José said to me.

29

Other sounds came. We saw more of Ada as José, already living at Ada's cousin's in town, was kept very busy in therapy and was then tutored at the school afterward. He learned to read his first grade primer and to write even before he could pronounce most of the words.

Six cases of congenital shortening of the frenum of the tongue were found and corrected. Doctor Suarez is writing a paper for a medical journal showing possible hereditary linkage as all the patients were somehow distantly related, as most people in Saint are, except one who was a godchild of a distant relative. Later, the cardinal listed them as Miracles Two through Seven, José's "miracle" being number One.

The rain lessened to a shower or two a day and the sun shone in between but the heat stayed away. Profits were holding at the store. The Spinning Marias' family additions kept growing. I was rarely consulted except for book work and for the new spring line, which I could not come up with. Classic or not classic, there are only so many ways to weave lace into bras, panties, and gowns. And I had long ago exhausted those possibilities. However I was more concerned with trying to sort out and figure out the hacienda's book work. With Pepe at my feet, I sat for hours in front of volumes of the Señora's firm but delicate script holding my head just so. If I held my head very still, I could focus without pain or distortion with the thick glasses. If I moved my head slightly, I had to start to focus all over again, which was why it was useless to drive or even walk with the glasses on.

The Spinning Marias finally stopped asking me for ideas for the spring line. These things are planned almost a year in advance. My inability to come up with even the simplest idea which they could then execute even into one new style began to bother me until it stuck like a pill in my throat. True, there was so much to concern myself with at the hacienda. But the store had always been mine — my sanity, my simplicity, my job.

It was one of the extra-terrestrials who initally suggested it. I was at the store after going to the hospital to get a progress report from Doctor Suarez for Ada.

"Rubia," the Spinning Maria with the now discreet hair net said, "since there will be no spring line..."

There was the pill in my throat — did she have to bring it up again?

"And since my brother who works at the hotel says that the Yankee oil companies have already been sending people in advance to check on living arrangements for the oil tourist families and since Señor Hernandez is retiring and has sugar in his blood and now his heart, and his son wants him to go and live with his family, he is selling the store and since it is right next door, we have thought we could buy it maybe and expand."

"*Las Imagenes de Santa*" had been in business long before "Isabella's Fine Lace and Linen" had become "Rubia's." It was a fairly small tourist shop which sold hand-painted plates and hand towels and placemats depicting the Blessed Virgin surrounded by floral rosaries and scrollwork marking festival names and dates or "there is no place like home" and the like. The owner Señor Hernandez was diabetic and had been complaining of his heart for years.

It would only be a small expansion, but on such a good street in the central shopping plaza, it would be an expensive one. But even if it showed a loss, it was a soothing solution to the lack of a new line. I went to see Señor Hernandez that week. His price was too high even for this district. He said, clutching his hand to his chest as always, that this price was not too high considering that he was throwing in all the plates, placemats, and hand towels. I told him that I only wanted the building and not the merchandise. But no, that was part of the deal and someone else might.

"Who paints these things?" I asked. They were as finely executed as they were tacky.

"Señora Vasquez, her two daughters sometimes, and sometimes her mother, when she is feeling up to it."

"Are they here? May I speak with them?"

There was something to the designs — something beyond the gaudy script and the Virgin Mother and the rococo swirls. I took off my glasses and examined them more closely — something in the delicate floral rosaries.

After the formalities were over, I asked Señora Vasquez if she had plans when the shop was bought out.

"Not exactly, Señora, but you are very kind to ask."

"Would you and your family like to work for me if I bought the shop?"

"Thank you, Señora, but I do not sew very well and I have never sold anything in my life."

"No, no, Señora Vasquez, you would still be painting. Not on the plates but on silk, with a little modification, of course, and I would pay very well."

"As long as I could still paint, it doesn't much matter who I paint for."

"And your daughters too?"

"I don't see why not, but I'll ask them."

They agreed. I bought the shop and donated the merchandise to the nuns to auction off at the next fund-raising bazaar. We bought the local stores out of silk and ordered more. The workmen gutted the new addition, fitted a workroom and removed *"Las Imagenes de Santa"* from the front door. There was some trouble with the color consistency of the silk dye lots. The Vasquezes practiced diligently on the silk remnants. I eliminated the Virgin and the scroll work. I rearranged the rosary bead formation into graceful sprigs and small clusters. The tiny delicate hand-painted flowers were as I had pictured them without my glasses. They were almost Oriental, almost English countryside, and unlike anything else. It was easy to transfer the lace pattern onto silk, keeping a minimal lace edge on some designs. I had only to add one new gown design — a white one, floor length, with one shoulder bare and the other featuring an ever so gentle sprig of "rosary" flowers in lavender. I also added some simple camisole tops to the line.

It was a pleasant change in the afternoon away from the tomes of hacienda ledgers where I spent the rest of my time deciphering.

"Remember," I told the Spinning Maria who smoked the little cigars who had taken over supervising the design execution. "Remember, simplicity is the key. I would rather ten less 'rosary' flowers than one too many." The Vasquezes had a tendency to be a little too heavy-handed but they soon caught on.

Production went well. A few prototypes were sent to New York. The samples were received well. Actual production was in progress so I spent less time at the store. I already had orders from New York and Paris when the Vasquezes decided to quit.

"Give them more money," I told the Maria with the hair net.

"That is not the problem, Rubia. They do not like the idea of putting something sacred on underwear."

"Lingerie, Maria, not underwear. But what's so sacred anyway. It's not like they're painting the Virgin herself on panties. It's only the flowers and hardly in the form of rosaries anymore."

"I've told them that. One of the daughters is willing to stay on maybe if I work on her a little more, but she could not possibly fill all the orders. Perhaps we can use stencils if we enlarge the design just a tiny bit."

"Oh no, Maria, hand-painted, no stencils, no enlargement even just a little. What the hell did they think they were going to paint — Rubia's Altar Vestments?"

The arguments went on for two days and two nights without me. Maria had begged me to let her handle it and to stay away after I told Señora Vasquez that the Virgin had tits too and would have liked to wear one of these bras had they been available at the time.

It became too difficult to stay away. When I finally stormed into the shop, everything was tranquil and busy.

"What happened?" I whispered to the Maria whose feet always hurt who was in the backroom making lace edges.

"Maria gave them a raise which they are contributing to the Church."

"Oh."

I have much to learn still.

I got Margherita a bra, although she still didn't need one, with little "rosary" flowers painted on the cups. She got her period shortly afterwards.

"I thought you told me you got this when you were older," Margherita said as if I had betrayed her. "You told me this happened to grown-ups."

She clenched her fists. Tears sprang to her eyes. Her hormones raged on:

"If this is so natural, if all women get this period, do the nuns get it too? I don't think they get it."

I was very tempted to tell her that no, the nuns don't get it. If you were destined for life in the convent, you wouldn't start to bleed every month. That's how you really know if you have a vocation or not.

"Yes, Margherita. It is perfectly natural. The nuns get it also."

"Oh, all right," she said a little calmer.

It was difficult but not impossible for me to finally decipher the various hacienda accounts and relatively easy to figure out who was in charge of what, but I could not always figure out *why*. If I was to make any kind of improvement, I had to figure out what was going on in the first place. There seemed to be century-old verbal agreements which even the people involved were not sure of. That left Rosa many times as the person I had to squeeze information from. Rosa had always had a good head for historical gossip. My "materialist questions" greatly annoyed her spiritualistic existence especially on Bingo nights as she had developed a burning passion for anything church-sponsored from novenas to fund-raising to Bingo. But getting information from Rosa wasn't exactly a pleasant experience for me either.

"Rosa, why does Ramon Ugarra oversee the planting on the west end?"

"Because that is his job."

"I understand that, but I cannot find any record of his salary."

"No, I think he took over his father-in-law's work when he died."

"Yes, but how does he eat then?"

"With his mouth like everyone else, Rubia."

"Very funny, Rosa. I am only asking you this because I cannot figure this one out from the books.'

"Not everything is in the books, Rubia."

"I know that, that's why I'm asking you."

"He eats."

"Well, then, how does he pay the rent?"

"There is no rent on Ramon Ugarra's house because of an agreement through his father."

"I thought you said the father was dead."

"No, I said the father-in-law was dead. The father is dead also. Ramon is no youngster himself, Rubia."

And then Rosa would go to church.

Juan Ortega squeezed back into his tight black pants and booked parade and club dates around the country. We did not see much of him. When he was home, he was dieting or whoring, which kept him out of the house.

The Señor and Federico spent long days with the horses. They made plans to enlarge the stables. What had only been a sideline of the hacienda, a passionate hobby of Señor Rodriguez, was being turned into an enterprise. It was good for my father-in-law. His eyes weren't exactly smiling again, but they were no longer lifeless. Federico lost the pounds around his stomach. When the rain slacked off to only a brief shower in the morning and one around sundown, his skin darkened with the sun and he looked healthy and strong again.

I started a separate account for the horses. It was a pleasure to have one account, one book from scratch, one book that did not require hours of delving into the past to figure out. They hired another trainer. They bought, sold, bred, broke in and trained. They lost money. I did not interrupt except to find answers that I could not find in the books regarding the lumber which was still the mainstay of the hacienda: What was the flood line on this piece of land or what was the harvesting date on that piece of land? The horses went into heat. Federico became less of a stranger. It was nice after I got used to the new positioning, and we didn't have to look at each other.

I was very sincere about making reforms on the hacienda. First I decided to compile a list of all those living on the hacienda along with their ages and occupations so I could initiate a salary and insurance plan. It was the first list of employees, full- and part-time, salaried and unsalaried, that had ever been compiled. The work was exhausting. Every time I thought the list was complete, I would have to check through hospital and church records to verify ages. When that was completed another baby would be born or some one would remember another old person living quietly in a back room who used to cut trees or plant vegetables. Then another person would remember a group of people or a tribe of Indians living upstream who could not be reached but who stripped trees and sent them downstream when the water level rose. Everyone was very cooperative. The list was never completed.

I then decided to initiate a group payroll plan since very few of the workers appeared to receive a salary.

I consulted Federico first.

"There is enough money, no?"

"Yes, and I will start with only those who take care of the wood, first, to simplify matters. It will take six months to a year for everyone else."

"If you think it is better, Rubia. My mother always wanted to make the place more modern."

"Your father, do you think I should consult him?"

"You can ask him, if you feel it is necessary, but I am sure he will not mind as long as it wouldn't affect the horses."

I thought everyone would mind. I thought other landowners would be angry at my example. I thought the workers would mind when I would start to take away years of unwritten agreements until they got used to a system of organized fair and just salaries. I thought the Church would mind for breaking tradition. But no one minded and the system failed miserably. Each first of the month payday wreaked havoc. Some took their wages and left. Most stayed and enjoyed a week-long celebration which they said had been initiated in honor of the Señora since enough time had passed since her death. When the payroll money was spent after a week, they would return to work.

Each month, the payroll celebrations grew. Songs were sung in the Señora's honor. Dances were danced in the Senora's honor.

And miracles. A woman conceived after twenty years without children — she had been wearing underwear with "rosary" flowers painted on it. I was tempted to recall the whole line. Miracle number 39, the cardinal would later note. A lame foot suddenly healed while dancing in the Señora's honor (number 57, the cardinal would later note).

When the last payroll celebration reached monumental proportions and closed down the city. Federico found me crying in the bedroom.

"Payroll is not that important, Rubia. Come and join the dancing."

"I can't," I told him, tears streaming down my face, "I know that payroll isn't that important but I can't."

"Well, then is it because of the tales and stories about my mother's miracles? People talk. It will pass. It bothers me sometimes too. I hardly recognize who they are talking about. It is not that important. Nobody really believes them. You don't believe them. Come."

"Of course I don't believe them!"

"Then come and dance."

Federico whispered in my ear while we danced. And I *wanted* to believe every word he said.

Ramon Ugarra, overseer on the north end, came to me
the next week.

"With all due respect, Rubia, the wood harvesting season
is here and we cannot afford another week-long celebration
away from the harvest. Perhaps it would be better to go back
to the old system and abandon payroll at least now."

"How can I take away what has already been started?
Perhaps we can start paying by the week so there won't be all
this accumulation of wages at the end of each month."

"Señora Rubia, it won't work."

"Well, what *can* I tell them?"

"Tell them your mother-in-law *wished* it that way through
a miracle or something."

"Ramon, I am not perpetuating these myths. These are
the myths which enslave the people."

"Señora Rubia..."

I made the announcement the next day: "It was the Señora's wish on her death bed that the festivals in honor of her
name would not take place during the harvesting season as
this is the season for work only."

Payroll went back into planning. We were already late with
the harvest and lost some money because of it, so I leased some
obscure unwooded land to one of the oil companies to make
up for it.

30

My oldest daughter Margherita, namesake of the Señora, began to take her name very seriously after the Señora died. Everyone from the nuns to Ada was feeding her stories about how saintly her grandmother was, how blessed to be the granddaughter of such a holy woman, how privileged she was to share her name. Margherita kept a statue of the Virgin in her room always with fresh flowers and a candle. She asked me one day, while I was begging her to go outside and play, when they would make a statue of Abuela. It startled me; I could see the Señora then as I had that night in the garden with her white gown and long flowing hair. I could picture a larger-than-life statue like that in the garden among the roses. It was only after I remembered the Señora's advice to cut off Frederico's balls that I was able to bring things back into proportion, back to life.

"I will have to think of some way to honor her then," Margherita said, "when they make her a statue."

"Yes, now go play," I said. "Your Abuela would prefer you to be outside playing."

Miracle number 72 (the cardinal later noted) took place shortly afterwards when Margherita saw the moving Christ's eyes on the life-sized crucifix at the church. There had nearly been a riot there. It was a school day; the nuns called and told me they would have to call the police if my daughter didn't move soon. There was quite a crowd at the church, not only the entire grade school and a flotilla of nuns but word had already spread and parents had arrived, some joining in behind the transfixed Margherita, others forcibly carrying their children out of the church. It was very hot in the church. Patricia was throwing up when I saw her. Margherita was kneeling like a statue in prayer below the life-sized crucifix of Jesus, his eyes permanently half-closed.

It took me almost a half hour to move her. I knelt beside her and whispered how God would prefer her to move since there were too many people in the church and someone might get hurt.

She didn't answer. She was somewhere else, fading, fading, like I thought death was. Fading forever like I thought the Señora had. Except that the Señora didn't fade like that, didn't die like I thought she would. It had been more like she had phoned in reservations, packed her bags, and moved. It was my daughter who was drifting into eternity.

"But he's trying to talk, Mama," Margherita said finally in a little whisper. "That's why I have to stay here and pray. I know he looked at me and moved his eyes and now he's trying to tell me something. He's trying, Mama, like he's really in there inside of the statue and can't get out."

And I told her that she didn't have to move if she didn't want to, but that if she did move she would be showing God her faith that he could find her anywhere in the world and talk to her in her heart.

And she moved, stiff and exhausted, and fell asleep in the car on the way home.

The nuns deserted Margherita after that. They said she couldn't come back to school without a certificate of sanity. They wanted one for Patricia too whose only crime was to throw up in a hot crowded church.

Dr. Suarez recommended Dr. Rojo, a young child psychiatrist just setting up practice. Dr. Rojo said Margherita's

condition wasn't too serious, only that she needed regular therapy and more outside interests like a hobby or the like. My
mother advised me, long distance, to get her a piano. My
mother couldn't conceive of anyone being sane who didn't have
a piano. Patricia took up riding to get out of the house when
Margherita played. They both went back to school.

Margherita shows extraordinary talent on the piano. She
refuses to play songs though, only scales and chords. Dr. Rojo
said it wasn't important and was delighted by her progress.
Margherita did not like the nuns teaching her piano because
they wanted her to play waltzes. We went through twelve sec-
ular piano teachers in six months. Most just got tired of chords
and scales and Margherita quickly outgrew the others. Federico finally found a Señor Jiminez, who is seventy-two, alco-
holic and has never played the piano. He apparently was a
classical guitarist although I have never seen or heard him
play the guitar either. He loves theory and hates waltzes. He
teaches music, he says, not piano. Margherita adores him and
progresses rapidly under his gaze.
    "When will she play a song?" Ada asked as Margherita
pounded through the chromatic scales.
    "How can you stand it!" Rosa screamed as Margherita
scaled through advanced quaternary forms. "She can't even
play 'La Cucaracha.' When is she going to play a song?"
    Some of the exercises almost sound like a song, *almost*
reach a melody.
    "When she is ready for a melody, it will find her," Señor
Rodriquez said.
    Rosa has boarded up her part of the house that connects
to the main house. Wood, bricks, cement and layers of soundproofing separate her from Margherita's exercises. She even
takes her meals separately and has her own help—Isabella and

Louisa work over there now that Ada and her cousin are back here full-time.

"I can no longer tolerate the noise," she gave as her reason for her move to her side of the house, "nor can I tolerate your permissiveness in allowing your daughter to continue so." She boarded her part of the house about the same time that her eldest daughter at fourteen years of age was found making out with an American boy from an oil company family down at the game room of the Buena Vista Hotel. Rosa and her daughters come to visit every Sunday for dinner. Dressed in their Sunday best, they leave the side door of their part of the house and walk around to the front of the main house and ring the door bell.

31

≈ ≈ ≈ ≈ ≈ ≈ ≈ ≈ ≈ ≈ ≈

A nd Federico. Ah, Federico.

"Do you have to wear your glasses in bed!" he says as he mounts me from the rear. "What are you trying to do, get a better focus on the pillow?"

He pretended not to see the look on my face when they modernized and expanded the stables and José's back room was replaced by more stalls. He pretends not to hear when Rosa gives me news from church that Maria-Elena's mother got a letter from her cousin in Miami, where Maria-Elena sells lingerie in a very fashionable department store. "She is engaged to one of the managers and is doing very well," the news goes.

He said, "No, I don't mind Margherita's playing," on the day all the hammers were boarding up Rosa's side of the house in a maddening rhythmic counterpoint to Margherita's poundings.

"One madness for another. You are replacing one madness for another, but I do not mind. It is a lesser evil."

And he went out and found the piano teacher who does not play the piano, when we had run out of piano teachers who played the piano. Federico dressed in a suit and tie and escorted me to the school hall when Margherita gave a performance at a combined recital. "Minor Seventh Scale and Chord Changes for the Left Hand" was the piece she performed. He led the applause. No one else in the auditorium was sure she had finished. No one else was even sure she had begun, not having even lifted her right hand to the keys.

"No, I don't mind," he said when no one showed up for work after my payroll failures.

"No, I understand that it is important to rotate the madnesses for a better balance."

There are many silences between us. We do not look too closely to see things we do not want to see. Our arguments lack the passion they once had—we do not wish to touch places that are still scarred. But we are trying.

"When is the next Festival of the Payday of my Mother?" he asks when our guards aren't up. "I haven't danced in a while."

Sometimes he lifts up my glasses and steals a kiss beneath them.

32

The day they discovered the oil, I was in the kitchen trying not to listen to Margherita practice, the old dog sleeping at my feet. Ada was preparing her "Yankee" dish of chopped hot dogs, sauerkraut, and potato stew, which she still served like a sloppy joe over open-faced hot dog buns.

"Why do they make these rolls such a strange shape, Ada?" I asked.

"I don't know," she said.

Ramon Ugarra was out of breath at the door. His speech was disjointed. His hat was in his hand, which he kept waving, and his white pants were spattered with a dark greasy mud.

"Rubia, it is a miracle! You are needed at once. The men from the oil company are down at the stables with Federico. They have discovered oil on the land you leased to them at the southeast end in the very place your daughter, namesake of the Señora, said it would be!"

"My daughter? Ramon, my daughter is in the living room. If you stopped for a moment, I'm sure you could hear her too."

"Rubia, I don't mean that Margherita is down at the southeast end. I am not deaf, only that the oil at the southeast end is where the Virgin told your daughter it would be."

"The men from the oil company said that? My daughter's vision was under the crucified Christ not the Virgin, Ramon, and she never mentioned oil or never mentioned to me about Christ mentioning oil."

"It is only what the people say, Rubia. I don't know what the men from the oil company say. That is why Federico told me to get you for you to talk with the men from the oil company."

"Did Margherita ever mention oil to you, Ada? The Señora mentioned oil to me."

"On her death bed, no?" Ramon Ugarra said.

"Yes."

"*Dios mio,*" Ada said and crossed herself. "Maybe the people have the miracles mixed up, but it is a miracle just the same, no?"

"Please, Rubia, come."

I grilled Margherita later that afternoon while Señor Jimenez impatiently rolled his eyes and turned on the metronome.

"There was no Virgin, right?"

"No, it was Jesus, Mama."

"And did he give you any instructions regarding a fountain or a spring or oil?"

"No."

"Well then, where did everyone get this idea about finding oil where the Virgin told you it would be found?"

"I don't know, Mama."

"You don't know?"

"I don't know, Mama. It was so long ago, when I was a child. I hardly remember it at all."

"Margherita, it wasn't that long ago."

"But it was before the music. It was a long time ago that way."

"Calm down, Rubia," Federico said.

"But it is just perpetuating those miracle myths which enslave the people, Federico."

"What do you know? If dinosaurs put the oil there a million years ago or if the Virgin sent a telegram this morning, it's still oil and if you want to reform the hacienda and raise the economic level of the workers like you say, oil seems as good a way as any."

"Yes," I remembered, "the oil."

Miracle number 94, the cardinal later noted.

33

The jungle reclaims the land quickly. We keep the fields by the stables cleared. The area by the house and the main road we keep clear also.

"Is this how you pictured it, Rubia?" Federico asked.

"It's amazing! It's like living on a game reserve. I saw a herd of wild domesticated pigs today not more than a mile from the house."

He said this after philodendron with leaves over four feet wide had blocked the door to the house and I had to go down to the stable to get him to clear it away with a machete. The philodendron grows so quickly—I had just been down to the shop for the afternoon.

Almost everyone is gone now. Federico's work with the horses has not been interrupted too much. Most of the trainers stayed. "They are 'horse people,'" Federico said. "They are not interested in things that do not concern horses." They gathered most of the horses that were running loose or almost starving from the villages and brought them to the main stable where they are cared for and help keep the fields clear by grazing. Most of the other animals roam free or are already dead. Pepe suddenly came awake one day and is enjoying his second youth keeping stray cows and pigs away and barking his territorial rights.

Most of the villages, even those not far from the house, are ghost towns. There are some old people still in them who refuse to move. Some houses still have a mule tied to a tree or a chicken coop in the backyard, but not too many. First, only the men went to work with the oil company. Then as housing was built, the women and children followed. Those who did not move to the southeast end did not like living in such isolation, so they moved to town.

Rosa moved back or rather kept the soundproofing, but had Ramon tear down the walls and boards which separated her side of the house. Louisa and Isabella moved to the southeast end, so Rosa had no one to help her maintain a separate residence. Everyone eats here now too just like before. Juan Ortega comes less frequently to visit. Town looks just about the same except for more foreigners. Three of the Marias from the store moved with their families to the southeast end, which is a large town by itself now, they tell me. It is not so noticeable at the store. The Spinning Marias quietly replaced the missing Marias with members of their family. Business is going very well, only the Marias are now no longer in the majority there.

And at any time, there is enough money in my separate bank account for plane fare to anywhere in the world for the girls and myself, for Federico and his father, for Rosa and her girls, for Ada and her cousin and her cousin's parents, for Señora Jimenez, for Ramon Ugarra and his family, for the horse trainers and all the horses. Enough money to start all over again anywhere away from here, away from the heat and the rain.

There is plenty of money on the hacienda too. The profit from the percentage of oil from the leased land is very high. Some of it I have reinvested in the oil company and that also shows a high profit.

The profits also contribute to cancer research. Dr. Suarez feels that whatever combination of local cures and Brinkston cocktail that I had hit upon for the Señora might not just be symptomatic relief but a cure for cancer. He looks a little mad some days, following people around with little dried leaves and vials and droppers and a thousand questions.

"Are you sure you are not taking any of these drugs you are experimenting with, Dr. Suarez?" I asked him.

"Are you sure you weren't taking any of these drugs when you saw the Señora transformed in the garden, Rubia?" he answered.

I have this fantasy that when they find the cure, I will hear that the old Indian chief, the one who appeared in our kitchen doorway years ago, is dying from the "curse of the wood that rots from the inside." I will dress in something comparable to his flaming strings of ceremonial garb—maybe a white silk with silver threads—and make the twelve-day journey to his village to give him the cure. At least the favor will be returned. Perhaps he will tell me that it wasn't necessary, that he is already recovering and that the new miracle drug I have brought was the same thing he had in his leather pouch.

There is also plenty of money to keep up the horses which have been a losing venture from the start. "It takes a few years to become established. The stables are still in the investment stage, Rubia," Federico tells me except that I don't care if they ever turn a profit. It keeps Señor Rodriquez's eyes bright and Federico busy. Patricia rides fairly well and has shown horses in the junior division already. The horses could eat gold nuggets and shit them in the fields if they wanted to. There is enough money and I wouldn't care.

The land is not money as the Señora had told me. The land is only jungle. I have not sold any. There is no need to. The precious wood is no longer harvested and we had to make good on some of the trade agreements we reneged on. The wood grows. The wood rots. The wood gets lost in the jungle. During the rainy season, the jungle spreads like fire. In days, there is jungle where houses had been or where I thought they had been.

"It doesn't bother me," Señor Rodriquez said. "I hear everyone is doing very well with the oil company. It's not your fault that everyone left. This is how I pictured the land would be when my wife died. This is how I pictured the land was before I was born. Before my grandfather was born."

Rosa's girls huddle in a corner and whisper after dinner. The change has affected them. They seem to have lost their pleasant simplicity. They appear wide-eyed and fearful, like fallen princesses, although this could have been caused by living so long boarded up with Rosa and not because of all the changes on the hacienda. I spend less time at the shop now. Rosa spends less time at church. No more Bingo, she only goes to mass each morning. She is afraid to go out except under God's protection to mass, she told me. "It is like a jungle out there!" Ada and her cousin go about their business. Rosa clings to me like a vine. We play Scrabble a lot. Rosa is the only one who will play with me. Sometimes we play in English. Sometimes in Spanish. Sometimes she plays in Spanish and I play in English. We argue a lot and I can no longer remember which are the English words.

"'Fumpt' is too a word," I told her. "It's English and it's dirty. You want me to give you the definition?"

"Don't bother," she said, "you always had a bad mouth."

When the rainy season ended, the jungle slowed its pace on land reclamation. The horses were in heat. Federico was exhausted working in the stables from dawn till dusk. At night, he kept me up for hours from behind. After one such session, I went down to the store in the morning to sleep without Rosa bothering me every few seconds. I was there when they called me to say that Federico had been in a minor accident at the stable when one of the horses had kicked in a fence. It was not serious they told me—the horse had not touched him and the fence barely grazed him, not even enough to break the skin. I met Federico at the hospital. They x-rayed him. They checked him on the most modern equipment. They sent him to specialists. They sent him to physical therapy. They said that time would heal whatever it was that was making him limp. When time didn't heal, they started all over again. There were no broken bones, no bone or muscle disease, no muscle damage, no internal bleeding, but they could not get rid of the limp.

It did not hurt, Federico said. But it was a pronounced limp.

"Stop worrying about it," my father-in-law told me. "It doesn't hurt him and he can still work. I have been all my life with a limp that hurts and it never held me back."

"There is *no* physical damage, but it is not psychological either," the doctors told me. "Even under total anesthesia, we cannot straighten the leg out."

Federico finally stopped the treatments, stopped trying to find out the reason.

"Please go to the doctor," I begged. "This is a new doctor."

"This is ridiculous, Rubia. I'm sorry that it upsets you so much, but it doesn't bother me and I'm not going to any more doctors. I have much work to do and it's a waste of time."

"Why do you want to be a cripple?" I screamed at him over and over again. "Why now? You have no scars. You have two good balls. Why do you persist limping?"

"Why do you think my balls have anything to do with it? I do not know why you have been so hysterical about this, but I can't waste any more time over it."

Only Ada seemed to realize its significance, although I never revealed it to her. I never told anyone about my aborted attempt to give my husband a limp. I would never tell anyone. Only the Señora knew and she had carried that secret with her to the grave.

"*Dios mio,*" Ada said. "I am praying as hard as I can for a miracle for his limp."

Except that the miracle had already taken place.

I went up to the Señora's room one afternoon after finally accepting the fact that Federico limped and would continue to limp for no known medical or psychological reason. There was not even a scar on his balls—I had inspected them again the night before with a magnifying glass after much protest from Federico.

The Señora's room was stripped except for the lace coverlet and a statue of the Virgin on the dresser. But the room did not seem empty. There was a votive candle in front of the Virgin which Ada lit when she dusted. I lit the candle for Federico's limp. Then I blew the candle out and let it be. Sun streamed through the window. I lay on the bed and stared at the little statue of the Holy Virgin, the original saint of the river.

"Dear Santa del Rio," I said to the lace coverlet, "or rather dear Señora, you lovely, lovely bitch." I fell asleep smiling.

Father Tomaso came up the road to the main house the next morning. A man dressed in a red cape and a red hat was with him.

"This is the cardinal, Rubia," Father Tomaso said. "He was sent from the capital on orders of the Vatican to investigate the sainthood of the Señora. The people have collected thousands of signatures attesting to her miracles."

The cardinal held his ringed hand out for me to kiss. I kissed it. "We have heard stories, Señora, that the deaf can hear, that the mute can speak, that illness has been cured, that the Señora Margherita has appeared to many in visions and that a cure for cancer in her name is being investigated by medical science. And also about the oil. We have heard that the Virgin appeared and directed the people to find oil in the Señora's name which has made them rich."

"It was Christ who appeared about the oil, Cardinal," I said, "not the Virgin."

"These are the details we have come to talk to you about," he answered.

"Come into the house then. I will give you every assistance."

I took off my glasses and lagging behind the cardinal and Father Tomaso, I dropped them into the mud and walked on them. I can hardly see without them. But perhaps on the day they declare the Señora a saint, the blind will see.

"I will compose a song when they make Abuela a saint," Margherita said. "A beautiful song. A symphony."

"That could be years, Baby. That could be hundreds and hundreds of years." I had already inquired as to when I could expect to see again. I asked the cardinal if the investigation was successful, how long till the proclamation of sainthood. He told me that it might be fifty years or many centuries. I could be blind for a long time.

"Do your song now, Margherita. Your Abuela is already a saint—there might not even be a world left by the time the Church makes it public."

"It doesn't matter," Margherita said. "I will wait for the announcement. I will be ready then."